Vampirology:

A Scientific

Study of

Vampires

Prologue:

My name is Steve Lehman, and this collection of data has been assembled through my efforts upon learning the following information:

1. Vampires do exist.

2. The teeth of vampires exist, and are extracted from deceased vampires.

3. The teeth, once extracted, are sought after either by the Roman Catholic Church for sanctification, or by other vampires (reason unknown at this time.)

I came upon a set of vampire teeth last year, and was able to conduct a few scientific experiments on said teeth before a collection of vampires took them. (This set of teeth was in my possession for seven days.) Since this original set of teeth were taken, I have put all of my resources into acquiring another set of vampire teeth while avoiding any attention from both the vampires and the Catholic church, both associations eager for me NOT to interfere with the status quo. (I compose this manuscript fully aware that I may be killed at any time while writing it.) All of the notes in this journal are from the second set of teeth.

Although I appreciate their desire for discretion, I am a scientist, and, as with everything else we can study, humanity needs to know as much as possible *ABOUT* as much as possible. As I am probably the only scientist who knows the three truths stated about, it falls upon me to learn about vampires, then to share this knowledge with whoever would like to learn from it.

Under conventional scientific settings, I would have performed a multitude of tests and experiments, following stricter scientific guidelines, and far better note taking. To stay one-step ahead of the church and the vampires, I moved my laboratory every other day to a new location, repeating a location every two weeks. With moving so frequently and dealing with the logistics of the moves, I elected to get as much data as possible whenever possible and publish it for the benefit of the human race.

Thus, this collection of data is what I have learned from studying the first set of vampire teeth and what I learned since acquiring the second set of teeth. I refer to myself as "the scientist" throughout the manuscript to lend a greater amount of professionalism to the material, and reduce the amount of personalization I experienced through the course of the experiments. However, I will be inserting side notes of random items I thought or observed during the experiments to establish the mental tone I was in at the time. I understand how many people will doubt the validity of these tests, and as well as my own sanity and stableness, for these readers are likely to be in the same area of disbelief about vampires as I was. I will also be inserting various scientific information to bring ordinary people up to speed on some of the scientific jargons, experiments, etc.

Validation of Test Materials

1) Upon acquisition of vampire teeth, the teeth were not removed from the packaging they were originally delivered in. At this stage of the study, there was no evidence that there were any teeth in the package. Working on the belief that the package did include a set of vampire teeth, every safety concern was practiced. The package was in a soft container, and did not have any warnings on the outside of it (Hazmat, flammable, etc.)

*Side note: The scientist found this lack of warning labels humorous, considering what was allegedly inside the package.

2) The package was deposited into a sanitized 10-gallon glass aquarium. A 10mm thick piece of steel was placed over the top of the aquarium. The fluorescent light fixture that originally adorned the top of the aquarium was placed in the back of the aquarium and turned on to provide observational light of the

package.

3) The package stayed inside the aquarium until a means of safely opening the package could be ascertained.

4) After 24 hours of observation, nothing appeared to change with the package. (A video recording of the package in this enclosure was reviewed to collect this information.)

5) After 48 hours, the scientist decided the best way to proceed with opening the package would be by using a glove box, a Plexiglas box with rubber gloves sealed to the hand ports for work with contamination-sensitive materials. The scientist ordered the box and it delivered two days later. During this waiting interval, the package did not alter from the previous 24-hour session.

6) The package was relocated into the glove box upon arrival of the unit. The video camera that was used to monitor the aquarium was now being employed to monitor the glove box. An Exacto razor blade knife

was used to remove the outer layer of the package. Once this initial wrapping was removed, the next layer was packaging straw. (Question for later research: why wasn't the package sent with bubble wrap?)

7) The Exacto knife was used again to peel away the packaging straw, which was approx 1.5" in thickness. An image began to take shape underneath the last remaining strands of the straw, at which time gloved hands removed the straw strands.

8) As the last of the straw was removed, a shiny object began to come into view. It appeared to be a silver eyeglass case as it was approximately the same size and shape of a case, as well as hinged on one side of the container. The case had a clasp on the opposite side of the hinged side.

> Side Note: At this stage of the experiment, the scientist removed himself from the box and reviewed the logic and theory of his next moves.

The scientist, more concerned about his own

safety after discovering the silver eyeglass case,

was processing whether or not the neoprene

gloves in the glove box would be strong enough

to resist any possible puncture attempts, if indeed

vampire teeth did reside inside the eyeglass case.

The neoprene was 30mil thick, a standard

thickness to repel acids and hypodermic needles.

The scientist knew to go to a thicker glove would

mean surrendering flexibility inside the case,

something the scientist believed was essential

during this initial opening. After a cup of tea, the

scientist resolved to continue with the experiment.

9) The scientist moved the packaging material to the far

sides of the box. He then undid the clasp and lifted

the lid to the silver case to discover two pointed teeth,

each tooth approximately 25mm long and 5mm wide.

The teeth had a mother of pearl look to them, and

appeared more like small pieces of carved marble

than a common human tooth. (The veins of the marble being a violet color.) The interior of the case was padded and covered with a blue crush velvet material. The case did not appear to have any dust or residue from the teeth. (This was later confirmed after review under an electron microscope.)

10) After this initial review of the teeth, they were placed back into the silver case and re-clasped. The scientist then prepared the glove box for photographing the teeth by taking the packaging material from the glove box and placing it into a separate container. Side note: The scientist was wearing a yellow haz-mat suit during this event.

11) After cleaning the glove box, the scientist could take photographs of the silver case; however, the teeth themselves did not appear in *any* of the photographs taken by the scientist.

(There are indents in the padding of the case where the
teeth resided.) Photos of the case are below:

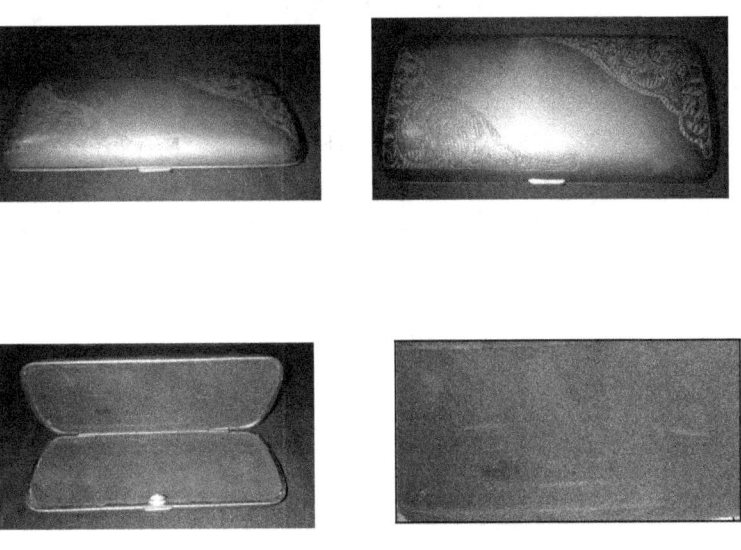

12) The scientist tried both digital and film photography;
neither media were able to deliver a photograph of the
teeth. The scientist later attempted to photograph the

teeth with an infrared camera. These photos did not illustrate the presence of anything besides a cold, blue background. Side note: The scientist considered providing a pencil illustration of the teeth, but decided against this. The scientists own artistic abilities are not very strong, and he does not feel comfortable endangering a qualified artist to such an unknown element.

The supplier of the vampire teeth has a famous and reputable reputation in the underworld/Gothic sub-culture of the occult. (The suppliers were also paid half of their installment upon delivery of the teeth to the scientist; the rest to be released from a bank account upon confirmation of the validity of the teeth.)

So how does one validate vampire teeth? Vampires are most associated with the sucking of blood for nourishment, so it would be logical to supply the teeth with blood and observe their reaction. However, there is also a safety concern with this as it is unknown what the reaction the teeth would have upon interacting with blood. Furthermore, the quantity, quality, temperature, and other unknown data about the blood to be provided makes this approach illogical.

The teeth disappearing in the photographs lend some genuineness to assuring the teeth are from a vampire, but another source of confirmation would be preferred. Exposure to sunlight, holy water, and other commonly believed vampire deterrents is an option, but such exposure may damage the teeth before further tests can be completed. Also, much like exposing the teeth to blood, there is an unknown safety factor concerning how the teeth will react when exposed to said deterrents.

Side note: This quandary left the scientist dumbfounded for many hours. After researching vampire lore on the Internet, the scientist developed a new experiment to authenticate the teeth.

<u>Mirror Experiment #1</u>

A defining attribute of a vampire is there lack of projecting a reflection with a mirror. Exposing the teeth to a mirror would be another form of confirmation with limited safety risk, the expected result being the teeth do not have a reflection when exposed to a mirror.

A basic glass mirror (size 30mmx60mm) was placed in the glove box beside the silver eyeglass container. The eyeglass container generated a reflection.

Upon opening the eyeglass case, the teeth were positioned as so both teeth could generate reflections on the mirror. Neither tooth generated a reflection.

The teeth were removed from the test area and each tooth was exposed to the mirror individually. Once again, no reflection.

The final test was the scientist picking up each tooth individually and exposing the tooth to the mirror while still holding the tooth in his gloved hand. The mirror reflected the neoprene hand, a transparent gap between the thumb and index finger that was holding the tooth.

Test 1: Hardness Test

Using a piece of equipment called a sclerometer, a comparison of the absolute hardness of minerals can be measured. The Turner-sclerometer test consists of microscopically measuring the width of a scratch made by a diamond under a fixed load, and drawn across the face of the specimen under fixed conditions.

The problem the scientist endured during the Turner-sclerometer test is such a scratch was never made by the sclerometer. In simpler terms, the diamond point could not make a scratch on either tooth.

There are two materials that are harder than a diamond: The first, wurtzite boron nitride, has a similar structure to a diamond, but is made up of different atoms. The second, the mineral lonsdaleite, or hexagonaldiamond, is made from carbon atoms just like a diamond, but they are arranged in a different shape. It is possible that one or both of these materials could scratch one of the teeth, but the scientist has his doubts that they would succeed where the diamond failed.

The first reason for this opinion is the strong similarities wurtzite and lonsdaleite compared to a diamond. Secondly, and perhaps more importantly, the teeth, have been not just physically altered, but mystically. Witnessing the failure of the diamond point to scratch either tooth, and understanding the mystical transformations the teeth must have endured when the original owner of the teeth became a vampire, it is doubtful anything of this Earth could scratch the teeth of a vampire. (wurzite and lonsdaleite tests permitting), vampire teeth are the strongest material on Earth.

Test Two: Separation

During the mirror experiment and the hardness test, the scientist discovered something peculiar about the teeth. When he would take one tooth for an experiment, the other would come along with it, as if pulled by an invisible string. The distance where the scientist noticed the teeth stopped pulling toward each other: approx 40mm, the same distance the two teeth would have been inside the previous owner's mouth.

It took some maneuvering inside the glove box to develop a way to work with one tooth at a time without the interruption of the second tooth. A piece of Plexiglas was cut to the dimensions of the inside of the glove box. When the scientist wanted to separate the teeth for the experiments, he would take a tooth and use the piece of Plexiglas as a temporary wall between the two teeth. There was still tension from the tooth being tested to rejoin with the other tooth, but the effort to maneuver the tooth being tested was minimal.

After the hardness tests, the scientist decided to study the nuances of this kinship between the teeth.

Test One, Variation One: Material for Separation

I. When one tooth was being examined on one side of the Plexiglas wall, the remaining tooth was against the other side of the Plexiglas. Furthermore, when the test tooth was moved upwards towards the ceiling of the glove box, the remaining tooth slid up the wall to the same height as the test tooth.

II. When one tooth was being examined with the remaining tooth still inside the silver eyeglass case, the scientist did not feel any tension from the test tooth. To insure there wasn't any tension at all from the test tooth, the scientist placed the test tooth on the floor of the glove box; no movement occurred.

III. With silver identified as a neutralizer for the pull of the two teeth, the scientist started testing other materials to discover if anything else could stop or reduce the pull of the teeth. The following is a list of the materials tested, and the results of said testing.

1. Paper: No alteration

2. Wood (14mm thick): no alteration

3. Salt*: no alteration

4. Sugar*: no alteration

5. Glass: no alteration

6. Cloth: no alteration

7. Steel: no alteration

8. Iron: no alteration

*To establish a barrier of these materials, the scientist built a wall from cubes/blocks of the material.

After these standard materials were tested, the scientist decided to delve into the mystical lore of vampires and observe if the teeth reacted to commonly-known vampire deterrents. These materials delivered much different results:

I. When a cross/crucifix was placed between the two teeth, the teeth reacted similarly as they did with the silver; no movement of attraction, even though there was a gab where the crucifix angled with the floor of the glove box.

II. When a line of Holy Water was spread with an eyedropper across the floor of the glove box, the two teeth once again reacted similarly as they did with the silver; no movement of attraction.

III. A cloth fragment from a priest's robe was

placed between the two teeth. Once again, no movement.

Test Three: Garlic

A common myth with vampires is their dislike for garlic. Garlic (Allium Sativum) has been used as a charm against evil and dates back the ancient Egyptians. They believed in a

Vampire-like ghost that killed sleeping children by sucking up their breath. The protection that was used against the attacks of this murderous monster was a wreath of garlic. In Romania, garlic is also a weapon of importance in the everlasting battle against Vampires. Romanians used to make certain that they ate garlic every day for their protection. They also smeared garlic on the windows and the doors of their houses, on the gates to their farmyards, and even on the horns of their cattle. They believed that these Vampires had a great fear of garlic. If a deceased person was thought to be in danger of becoming a Vampire one way of protecting them from turning was with garlic; they would shove garlic cloves up the deceased person's nose. This was done to prevent evil spirits from entering the dead body. Another anti-Vampire practice that we can find in Romania is the anointing of the corpse, especially the heels, with a mixture of oil, fat, incense, gunpowder, and garlic.

Many spiritual practices and religions believe that decalcifying the pineal gland (also known as the third eye) helps people who want to tune their spiritual antenna and refine their pineal gland. The pineal gland is a tiny pea-shaped gland located in the geometric center of the brain that is believed to improve health functions and self-awareness. It is believed by some Eastern and Earth based religions that garlic can detox and decalcify the pineal gland allowing for a sense of all knowing euphoria and oneness. This decalcifying process, per these ancient practices, is supposed to allow positive energies in the body and ward off evil spirits, which would likely include vampires.

Side note: The scientist had his doubts whether the teeth would react to the garlic. To begin with, the hardness of the teeth to diamond scratching made the likelihood of something as soft as garlic having any affect illogical.

Second, there is an opinion in the vampire world that the power of garlic against vampires stems from the pungent odor of the garlic cloves. The enhanced senses of the vampire are even more disturbed by the odors of the garlic, making vampires weak from the aroma of the cloves. It is illogical that a garlic smell would have any affect on something outside of a vampire nose.

Third, garlic is known for having high amounts of antioxidants and being a blood thinner, two things that vampires may not want in their dietary consumption. This distaste of garlic-laden blood maybe derived from a health viewpoint as well as the flavor of the blood.

Garlic Test #1

I.   A fresh clove of garlic was placed inside the glove box. The scientist opened the eyeglass case. No response from teeth.

II. The teeth were taken from the eyeglass case and placed closer to the garlic clove. No response from teeth.

III. The garlic clove was placed between the teeth. No response from teeth.

IV. The garlic clove was rubbed against one of the teeth. Scientist believed he felt a slight tremor from the tooth.

V. Scientist repeated experiment IV with the second tooth, this time holding the tooth with a pair of industrial tweezers rather than with his neoprene-gloved hand. This time the clove of garlic maintained contact with the tooth. The tooth shook loose from the tweezers.

Side Note: when more is known about the power of the teeth, additional tests should be conducted to measure the stress levels generated by the teeth.

Garlic Test #2

I. The experiments of Garlic Test #1 were repeated, with freshly diced garlic in place of the cloves. A small plastic container (20mL) of diced garlic was placed in the glove box, along with a bundle of q-tips to apply the diced garlic to the teeth.

II. Each tooth received a swipe from the diced garlic. The teeth trembled, but not as violently as when the teeth were touched with the garlic cloves.

Garlic Test #3

III. The experiments of Garlic Test #1 were repeated, with garlic powder in place of the cloves. A small plastic container (20mL) of garlic powder was placed in the glove box, along with a bundle of q-tips to apply the diced garlic to the teeth.

IV. Each tooth received a swipe from the garlic powder. No movement was observed.

V. Each tooth was placed directly into the plastic container of garlic powder. No movement was observed.

Garlic Conclusions

I. Garlic does have an adverse reaction with the vampire essence in the teeth.

II. Fresh garlic will have an adverse affect on a vampire; dried/aged garlic does not.

Garlic Theory

I. An unidentifiable element in the vampire teeth reacts to garlic. As that normal human teeth do not respond to garlic, it is logical to assume that the vampire essence in the teeth is what reacts to the garlic

II. Considering how the vampire teeth reacted to the garlic, it is logical to assume that an entire vampire entity would react similarly as the teeth, that reaction being one of rejection and evasion.

Garlic Questions

I. What chemical component makes vampires react to Garlic?

II. Why don't other known medical herbs have an affect on vampires?

Test Four:

Religious Items/Artifacts

There is a great deal of confusion and myth concerning vampires and Holy items. Many believe holding Holy objects, like a cross or Bible, will protect one from a vampire, the simple belief being vampires are evil creatures, so they will reject sacred items. (Some believe vampires will also resist sacred places for the same reason.) Some believe these artifacts/locations do not have to be exclusively Christian; that the symbol itself is not as important as the faith of the person using it.

From a scientific viewpoint, there is too much variability with these statements to create a reliable conclusion. For example, if the faith of a person is part of the equation, then the strength of the artifact/object is directly related to the faith quotient of the person holding it, which would mean that all religious items would be null in the hands of an atheist. Similarly, a cross would be useless in the hands of a person of the Jewish faith, as their religion does not identify Jesus as the son of God.

Side note: After observing the affects of the teeth with the cross during the separation test, the scientist will postpone further tests with the cross as to avoid possible damage to the teeth; other religious paraphernalia will be tested first.

Side Note: Any resistance from the religious items will not be forced past a certain point as to avoid any possible damage to the teeth, or other possible safety concerns. (The greater the amount of force against the resistance would require greater control than the neoprene gloves in the glove box can accommodate.)

Religious Items Test One

Various items of different faiths were obtained for this round of tests. The items were made of natural materials, or, if the items were hand made, then the object would be in their purest and simplest forms. The items include:

1. A Jewish Tallit (prayer shawl)

2. A Jewish Chai

3. An Islamic Crescent Moon and Star

4. An Islamic Shahada

5. A miniature Buddha statue

6. A Dancing Nataraja (Hindu)

7. An Ohm (Hindu)

8. A Bald Eagle Feather (A Native American Spiritual tool)

9. Rosary beads (Catholicism)

10. A Wooden Cross

The items were tested in the order listed above. Each individual item was placed in the glove box. The silver eyeglass case was opened, and the teeth were exposed to the items. No affects were noticed at various measurements until the teeth were 14 MM from the items. The affects of the teeth with the items above are listed below:

1. Buddha statue, Nataraja, Ohm, Bald Eagle Feather: No affect

2. Tallit, Chai, Crescent Moon, Shahada: Slight resistance felt.

3. Wooden Cross, Rosary beads: Intense resistance felt

The scientist expected the amount of resistance displayed when the teeth encountered the Cross. Considering the Rosary Beads are from the same religion as the Cross, the affects from the teeth when encountering the beads was not surprising, but not expected either.

The lack of resistance from the Ohm, Eagle Feather, Nataraja, and Buddha disproves the belief that any religious item will produce an adverse reaction with a vampire. (The scientist expected these results from these tests.)

The slight resistance felt from the Tallit, Chai, Crescent Moon, and Shahada surprised the scientist. This round of tests inspired the scientist to ask the following questions:

1. Why was there limited resistance from these non-Christian items?

2. The other non-Christian items did not stimulate any resistance, so why these four?

3. Might the material these religious items were made of cause the resistance?

4. Might the vampire from which the teeth were taken have a genetic disposition to the cultures aligned with these religious items?

Taking into consideration question #4 first, the scientist understood that he could not identify the origin of the teeth. Side note: upon reflection of this matter, the scientist also realized that throughout all the experiments he had assumed the teeth were male; no scientific evidence existed identifying the sex of the owner of the teeth. He would have to adjust his thinking and consider possible tests to make sex identification possible. The scientist doubted that there would be differences in the results of the tests he had conducted thus far if sexual identification would have been possible; he knew he would have to confirm these beliefs if he ever deduced how to ascertain the sexuality of vampire teeth.

Question #3 also arrived with doubts. The results from the separation tests revealed that the only material the teeth responded to without any mythological or spiritual connectivity was silver. The scientist understood there might be a percentage of the material in the second set of items that may be objectionable to a vampire, but he also understood that the items in section one that did not trigger any response from the teeth could also hold the same amount of objectionable material. Thus, from a logical viewpoint, this hypothesis did not equate.

After consideration and contemplation of these questions, the scientist deduced the answer for these questions must reside not in the world of the physical, but of the religious.

Religious Items: Test Two: Non-Christian Specific

The scientist repeated the sequence of events from Religious Items Test One, this time placing two items from the slight resistance test results together in the glove box simultaneously. The test delivered the following results:

    I.   Tallit and Chai: 14MM of resistance

    II.   Tallit and Crescent Moon: 14MM of resistance

    III. Tallit and Shahada: 14MM of resistance

    IV. Chai and Crescent Moon: 14MM of resistance

    V.   Chai and Shahada: 14MM of resistance

VI.   Crescent Moon and Shahada: 14MM of resistance

Religious Items Test 3: Non-Christian Specific

The scientist repeated the sequence of events from Religious Items Test One and Two, this time placing three items from the slight resistance test results together in the glove box simultaneously. The test delivered the following results:

1. Tallit, Chai, and Crescent Moon: 14MM of resistance

2. Tallit, Chai, and Shahada: 14MM of resistance

3. Chai, Crescent Moon, and Shahada: 14MM of resistance

Religious Items Test Four

The scientist repeated the sequence of events from

Religious Items Test One, Two, and Three, this time placing

all four items from the slight resistance test results together in

the glove box simultaneously. The test delivered the

following results:

I.   Tallit, Chai, Shahada, and Crescent Moon: 14MM of

      resistance

From the results of Religious Items Tests Two and

Three, the following conclusions may be true:

I.   Two items from the Jewish and Islamic faiths

      combine to create the same amount of resistance

      against a vampire as one Christian item.

II.   Three items from the Jewish and Islamic faiths do not

      increase resistance to a vampire.

III. Multiple items from the Jewish and Islamic faiths do

      not increase resistance to a vampire.

Religious Items: Test 5: Christian Specific

Up to this point, the scientist has focused on Non-Christian Items. With Religious Items: Test 5, the focus will be on Christian Items. Items testes in this experiment include:

I.   A cross

II.   Rosary Beads

III.   A scrap of a priest's robe

IV.   A scrap of paper from a Bible

Each individual item was placed in the glove box. The silver eyeglass case was opened, and the teeth were exposed to the items. No affects were noticed at various measurements until the teeth were 14mm from the items. The results from each of the four Christian items were the same: 14mm of heavy resistance.

Religious Items: Test 6: Christian

Specific

The scientist repeated the sequence of events from Religious Items Test 5, this time placing two Christian items together in the glove box simultaneously. The test delivered the following results:

I. Robe Scrap and Bible Scrap: 28MM of heavy

     resistance

II. Robe Scrap and Cross: 28MM of heavy

     resistance

III. Robe Scrap and Rosary Beads: 28MM of heavy

     resistance

IV. Rosary Beads and Bible Scrap: 28MM of heavy

     resistance

V. Cross and Bible Scrap: 28MM of heavy

     resistance

VI. Cross and Rosary Beads: 28MM of heavy

     resistance

Religious Items: Test 7: Christian Specific

The scientist repeated the sequence of events from Religious Items Tests five and six, this time placing three Christian items together in the glove box simultaneously. The test delivered the following results:

I. Cross, Bible Scrap & Robe Scrap: 42MM of heavy resistance

II. Cross, Rosary Beads & Bible Scrap: 42MM of heavy resistance

III. Bible Scrap, Robe Scrap & Rosary Beads: 42MM of heavy resistance

IV. Rosary Beads, Cross & Robe Scrap: 42MM of heavy resistance

Religious Items: Test 8: Christian Specific

The scientist repeated the sequence of events from Religious Items Tests 5, 6, and 7, this time placing all four Christian items together in the glove box simultaneously. The test delivered the following results:

I. Bible Scrap, Rosary Beads, Cross, Robe Scrap: 56mm of heavy resistance

Religious Items: Test 9: Christian and Non-Christian Specific

The scientist repeated the sequence of events from Religious Items Tests 5, 6, and 7, this time placing a Christian item with a Non-Christian item. Rather than quote each combination, the scientist will simply report that the resistance was not enhanced or reduced past the 14mm resistance reported by the single Christian Item.

Religious Items: Conclusions

- Each time a Christian item was combined with another Christian item, the resistance from the teeth increased.

- The addition of non-Christian items did not affect the resistance factor of the Christian item.

- The scientist cannot confirm that the distance between the

Christian Items and a complete vampire would be the same.

- It is logical to believe that the same level of resistance to the items would be the same for a complete vampire.

Religious Items: Theories

1. The vampire teeth can determine the religious orientation of a religious item. Thus, it is logical to assume that a complete vampire has this ability.
2. The religious orientation of the person brandishing the religious item would not be relevant to a vampire.

Religious Items: Questions

1. Do Christian/Catholic religious items have a stronger affect on vampires because Dracul, according to lore, blasphemed against the church to become a vampire?
2. What would be the affect on a vampire if a religious item

were composed of silver, garlic, or some other known vampire deterrents?

Test 5: Holy Water

A popular vampire lore is the employment of holy water as an apotropaic, the belief being contact with holy water will burn a vampire as if the holy water were acid. Some also believe that if a vampire were to ingest holy water, the holy water would burn through the vampire's insides, thus killing the vampire.

From a scientific viewpoint, does anything happen to water that has been blessed?

Furthermore, what constitutes "holy" water; what must be done, and by whom, to create such a combination? A common holy water creation is water that has been blessed by a member of the clergy or a religious figure, but what constitutes a religious figure? Also, there are various ranks within different religions; does this affect the potency of the water once it is transformed?

Per the topic of holy water in various faiths, the following are a few instances where holy water/blessed water are acknowledged:

- In Ancient Greek religions, holy water called chernips (Greek: χέρνιψ) was created when a torch from a religious shrine was extinguished in it. Also, purifying people and locations with water was part of the process of distinguishing the sacred from the profane.

- Sikhs use the Punjabi term amrita for the holy water used in the baptism ceremony known as Amrit Sanskar or Amrit Chhakhna.

- The idea of "blessed water" is used in virtually all Buddhist traditions. In the Theravada tradition, water is put into a new pot and kept near a Paritrana ceremony, a blessing for protection. This "lustral water" can be created in a ceremony in which the burning and extinction of a candle above the water represents the elements of earth, fire, and air. This water is later given to the people to be kept in their home.

- Most Mahayana Buddhists typically recite sutras or various mantras (typically that of the bodhisattva Avalokitesvara for example) numerous times over the water, which is then either consumed or is used to bless homes afterwards. In Vajrayana Buddhism, a Bumpa, a ritual object, is one of the Ashtamangala, used for storing sacred water sometimes, symbolizing wisdom and long life.

- The drinking of "healing water" (ab-i-shifa) is a practice in various denominations of Shia Islam. In the tradition of the Twelve Shia, many dissolve the dust of sacred locations such as Karbala and Najaf and drink the water as a cure for illness, both spiritual and physical. The Ismaili tradition involves the practice of drinking water blessed by the Imam of the time. This water is taken in the name of the Imam and has a deep spiritual significance. This is evident from the names used to designate the water, including light (nūr) and ambrosia (amṛt, amī, amīras, amījal). This practice is recorded from the 13th and 14th centuries and continues to the present day. The ceremony is known as ghat-pat in South Asia. (SIDE NOTE: Wuzu water is not holy water as lay people use it to prepare for prayer. Also, Zamzam water was not used in the tests as there is no way the scientist could verify that the water is genuine zamzam water.)

The scientist reflected about the different religious waters. The religious item tests showed that certain items of specific faiths had an affect on the teeth; would the religious waters also have the same results.

Oddly, the easiest water to acquire (outside of Catholic Holy Water, which is available at any Catholic church in the world) was Chernips. In ancient Greece, purification of the self was required before approaching the Gods, including entering the temples.

Using chernips is symbolic of the Water washing away míasma (pollution). The use may seem similar to the basin of holy water found near the door of Catholic churches, but chernips represents ritual cleansing, where the Christian holy water has more of a connotation of a blessing.

On one level, we wish to be in an appropriate state when approaching the Gods through ritual, so we literally want to be physically clean and show due respect to the Gods, but ultimately, the act of washing hands is symbolic of attaining a type of purity which cannot be secured by the act alone. Nonetheless, using chernips is a skillful tool to help us change our attitude. At the very least, we try, we attempt to be pure of heart, even if we cannot quite accomplish this change; our intention is to leave the profane behind.

Side note: Upon learning this material, the scientist pondered the concepts of purity and profane in connection to vampires. Might purity be the component that vampires reject when it comes to the topic of holy water? Might this be the variable if there is a variation between religious items and holy water?

The scientist also found the idea that in ancient Greece a layperson could create holy water:

Distilled water, although very pure, is not quite appropriate. The ideal water would be that which is obtained from an unpolluted, flowing spring or from the ocean in an area where it is clean. If these are unavailable, use bottled spring-water. If you cannot afford bottled spring-water, tap-water is sufficient.

Light a candle and dedicate this

candle to Hestia. Now, obtain fire
from the Hestía-candle using a
toothpick or similar; this flame
represents the Fire of Life, the
possession of the Goddess.
Extinguish the fire in the water
saying a simple prayer, something
like this:

> "Come Queen
> Hestía, Goddess
> of the Hearth.
> Remember the
> offerings we
> have given to
> you in the past
> and make this
> water chernips!"

The scientist conducted the ceremony as stated above and
poured it into a ydrána (suitable vessel).

Obtaining the waters from the other various faiths proved difficult. Purchasing religious items was easy; the internet has many sites selling such things. Acquiring genuine holy water proved much harder. Romania is 85% Christian, and although there are Buddhists and Muslims in Romania, there are only a few cities in the entire country that have those faiths. Furthermore, being an outsider to the faiths in question, he didn't feel it would be appropriate to just enter their places of worship and ask for their holy water; acquisition of these holy waters would require some significant maneuvering. (***Side note: Due to its length, the story of how the scientist obtained the Islamic and Buddhist waters is included as an appendix to this journal.)

The four holy waters employed in this series of tests include:

1. Abi Shifa (Islamic)
2. Chernips (Ancient Greek)
3. Catholic
4. Lustral water (Buddhist)

These waters were analyzed for micro organisms, pathogens, pesticides, sulfur compounds, iron, copper, lead, manganese, and other assorted contaminates that are common in water. All four of the holy waters tested would have been deemed acceptable for household use, the only variant being water hardness, which varies from well to well. For these experiments, the scientist decided that the holy waters did not possess any contaminates that would persuade the results of the tests.

Along with the holy waters, the scientist included the following waters for review:

1. Distilled water
2. Ocean-grade salt water

Holy Water: Test 1

A 2 oz. Plastic cup of one of the test waters was placed inside the glove box. Beside the plastic cup were several test swabs (q-tips). A tooth would be removed from the eyeglass case and placed near the plastic cup to identify for possible reaction to the water being near it. Side note: the tooth did not show any reaction to being near any of the waters.

A test swab was immersed in plastic cup of water. The swab was removed from the water and allowed to drip any excess water back into the cup. The damp swab was then placed onto the tooth for a maximum of 5 seconds. The tooth laid on the floor of the glove box during the test to observe for any possible movement Side note: some of the test waters did not require 5 seconds to register a test result.

The following test waters delivered these results:

1. Distilled Water: No noticeable result

2. Salt Water: No noticeable result

Holy Water: Test 1A

- For each individual experiment, a 10 oz. Plastic container of the Abi Shifa water, Lustral water, and Chernips were placed inside the glove box. Each holy water was tested against the vampire teeth.

- A test swab was immersed in plastic cup of each of the holy water(s). The swab was removed from the water and allowed to drip any excess water back into the cup.

- The tooth laid on the floor of the glove box. The damp swab touched the center of the tooth for less than a second. This slight touch caused the tooth to spin in a clockwise rotation, as if it were a gear inside a clock. The spinning was not fast enough to cause a blur, but more of a teetering motion. After 4 seconds, the spinning came to a halt. After waiting 30 seconds to take notes and to observe for any other possible delayed reactions, the tooth was reviewed for any possible damages; no damages appeared on the tooth. (These results were similar for each of the holy waters tested.)

- A second test of the three holy waters was altered to allow a drop of the holy water to fall onto the tooth. Once again, the tooth spun in a clockwise rotation, once again for approximately 4 seconds.

Holy Water: Test 2

- A 10 oz. Plastic container of the Catholic Holy

Water was placed inside the glove box.

- A test swab was immersed in plastic cup of each of the holy water(s). The swab was removed from the water and allowed to drip any excess water back into the cup.

- The tooth laid on the floor of the glove box. The damp swab touched the center of the tooth for less than a second. This slight touch caused the tooth to shake and emit a vapor. Upon removal of the test swab, the tooth showed intense purple coloring in the veins of the tooth. There was also a roughness to the texture of the tooth where the test swab had touched the tooth.

Holy Water: Test 3

1. The purpose of experiment is to ascertain if Holy water, when heated to the point it becomes steam, still retains its Holy status and is still employable as a vampire deterrent.

2. As that Christian Holy waters displayed the strongest test results from both Holy Water tests I & II, it was the only Holy water used during this experiment.

3. One of the factors to be considered during this experiment is the intensity of the steam. To fulfill this test, the entire glove box will have to be filled with various levels of Holy Steam. While the Holy Water was liquid, it was 100% water; when the Holy Water is turned to steam, it will only create a percentage of the air in the glove box. A humidity monitor will measure the amount of "Holy Humidity" in the glove box.

4. A beaker filled with holy water was heated via a Bunsen burner. The Steam from the beaker was transported to the glove box via a hose that was inserted into the vapor test port in the glove box.

5. The glove box was heated to a temperature necessary to maintain the steam in a vapor form. The humidity monitor dictated the temperature needs of the

experiment.

Side note: This experiment was approved by the scientist after observing the regeneration process of the teeth when provided blood. The scientist hypothesized that since the roughness and the mark from prior experiments healed from exposure to the mouse's blood, it was logical that the tooth would also heal from any possible injury from this experiment as well. However, as this was just an educated theory, only one tooth would be used for this experiment.

6. The Holy humidity amount in the glove box created the following results

   o From 10% to 50%, no alteration was observed.

   o From 50% to 60%, the purple veins in the tooth began to thicken (as it had during other experiments.)

   o At 60%, the scientist thought he saw a small

growth appear on the tooth. This growth increased in size each time the humidity increased till it reached 2mm in size.

- o While the humidity level was increasing, a second growth appeared on the other side of the tooth. It also appeared that the tooth began to have miniscule bumps appear sporadically on the tooth.

- o The bumps could best be described as blisters, although the scientist could not indentify what the interior of the bumps consisted of. The bumps were of a dark violet color, similar to the same hues the veins of the teeth displayed while under states of duress during previous experiments.

- o The scientist wanted to increase the humidity level to a percentage that may have caused the bumps to explode. He decided against this though, unsure of what such an event would do to the tooth, as well as what would happen to the area of the explosion after the humidity level was reduced. Furthermore, the remnants from the implosion would create an unclean glove box for further experiments; every experiment after the explosion would have to be noted for possible contamination from the implosion particles. Also, although unlikely, there was also the chance that the explosion could crack the glove box.

Holy Water Conclusions

1. Holy Water has an affect on vampire teeth.
2. Different holy waters from different faiths have different affects on the teeth.

Holy Water Questions:

1. Can a vampire sense holy water before it is opened? (Can a vampire sense a container of holy water while the water is still inside the container?

2. Can the strength of the Holy Water increase if it is stored in a Holy relic/container?

Holy Water Theories

1. Since Vlad Dracula, abandoned Christianity and Catholicism, it stands to logic that Holy Water from these two faiths would impose the most damage to a vampire.

2. As that Judaism and Islam share many beliefs, origins, historical events, it would be logical to assume that these similarities with Christianity are what make the holy waters from these faiths repulsive to vampires.

Test 6: Sunlight

Vampire lore is riddled with a common belief of vampire's objection to sunlight. Some beliefs state a vampire will catch on fire. Some beliefs state a vampire will explode from within. Still others believe sunlight will not have any affect on a vampire.

To coincide with these various beliefs are various remedied vampires use to avoid sunlight:

- Total coverage of the skin when exposed to sunlight
- Application of SPF 50 skin cream, which filters out up to 98 percent UV radiation. (There is no evidence that the 2% difference has any affect on a vampire.)
- The wearing of motorcycle helmets with UV visors.

With so many variables with the beliefs concerning sunlight and vampires, the scientist decided to experiments with the affects of UV light on the teeth in the controlled setting of his laboratory. The scientist decided against exposing the teeth directly to sunlight until more data could be obtained. (The scientist also knew how difficult and expensive it would be to acquire replacement teeth, in the event they were destroyed during the testing process.)

Black Light Test 1

With the black light generating 365nm, the scientist employed UV filters of 100, 200, and 300nm, thus reducing the amount of UV exposed to the teeth to 265, 165 and 65nm, respectively. Without having the data available of what happens to the teeth when exposed to sunlight, the scientist chose to expose one tooth at a time to the black light. The scientist would study the affects of UV rays on both teeth after he acquired preliminary data of the affects of the black light on one tooth.) Unless there was an affect on the first tooth exposed to the UV rays, he would not test the second tooth.

As stated above, a tooth was removed from the eyeglass case and placed inside a velvet bag. The black light was expensive it was for him to obtain the set of vampire teeth he had and did not want to risk destroying these items.)

Ultraviolet (UV) light is an electromagnetic radiation with a wavelength from 400nm (750THz) to 10nm (30PHz), shorter than that of visible light but longer than X-rays. The amount of UV light reaching the ground in any given place depends on many factors, including the time of day, time of year, elevation, and cloud cover. To help people better understand the strength of UV light in their area on a given day, the UV Index was developed, which grades the strength of the rays on a scale from 1 to 11+. A higher number means greater risk of exposure to UV rays. UV rays are strongest between 10 am and 4 pm., and grow stronger as the elevation increases.

For the purposes of the sunlight experiments, a mercury-vapor black light will be used. A mercury-vapor black light generates a peak of 365nm of UV light. Sunlight hits the Earth's surface at 700nm. The ozone layer, the time of day, time of year, elevation, and cloud cover diffuse these UV rays to various amounts. The mercury-vapor black light should suffice as a sunlight substitute as it is equal to 52% of sunlight UV, a comparable amount of UV that can be reduced from sunlight UV after all of the diffusing considerations.

Different UV diffusing filters will be employed to gauge

how much UV light affect the vampire teeth, if indeed it is UV light that is the source of the vampire deterrent in sunlight. Black lights do not generate much heat (as compared to, say, a halogen light.) Due to the lack of heat generated by black lights, clear filters of different gauge can be slipped over the black light bulb. (Side note: There are two main UV film filters for lights: amber and clear. Amber filters are better for UV rays over 400nm, clear filters are better for under 400nm, with an end point of 200nm.)

Supplying electricity to the glove box for said tests proved difficult, as the glove box did not have an access ports for the wiring. The scientist drilled a hole in the base of the glove box, inserting a rubber wire gasket in the drilled hole to secure the wire and limit outside exposure to the interior of the box.

Then came the issue of how to conduct the test. Should the black light be on and at full power before opening the silver case? This approach would expose both teeth to the black light at the same time, the one thing the scientist wanted to avoid until the second round of tests. A tooth could be taken from the eyeglass case and placed aside till the light was turned on, but then the tooth would be exposed to the light while it was charging, thus the results of the would have to reflect this time lapse.

The scientist elected to take one tooth out of the case and place it in a small velvet bag. (Velvet was chosen as the cloth of choice to limit possible light exposure.) The light would then be turned on with the tooth being exposed once the light was at full strength. Fitted with the filter required for the specific test, and then turned on.

1. **<u>Black Light Test with 300nm Filter</u>**: Without having any knowledge of the possible affects of UV rays on the test subjects, the scientist elected to expose the first tooth to the minimum amount of UV rays possible in this initial test. The tooth was placed in the velvet bag as described, with the black light being turned on immediately after. The tooth was removed from the bag with tongs and exposed to the

UV rays from the black light.

Test Results: Over the time of ten seconds, the violet veins of the tooth appeared to thicken and darken. Side note: The tooth did not tremor as it had during the Garlic test. The second tooth was removed from the eyeglass case as so both teeth could be exposed to the 300nm filtered light. The same thickening and darkening affect occurred in the second tooth, in a similar amount as the first tooth. (It took 5 seconds for the tooth to return to normal condition once the light was turned off.)

2. **Black Light Test with 200nm Filter**: The test was conducted similarly to the prior test, the only alteration being the replacement of a 200nm filter for the 300nm filter.

Test Results: Over the time of ten seconds, the violet of the tooth thickened and darkened again, both affects increasing approximately twice the amount as the first test. Side note: It took 10 seconds for the tooth to return to normal condition once the light was turned off.

3. **<u>Black Light Test with 100nm Filter</u>**: The test was conducted similarly to the prior test, the only alteration being the replacement of a 100nm filter for the 200nm filter.

<u>Test Results</u>: The violet veins of the tooth thickened and darkened again, this time encompassing the entire tooth to the point the tooth appeared inverted from the regular appearance of the tooth. The white area was the size of the initial purple veins, and a dark purple color replaced the lighter violet color of the   original veins. The new color had almost encompassed the entire tooth. Side note: It took 30 seconds for the tooth to return to normal condition once the light was turned off.

<u>Sunlight Conclusions</u>

1. Ultra-violet light had an affect on the vampire

teeth.

2. The greater the amount of UV rays, the greater the affect on the teeth.

Sunlight Theories

1. The vampire element inside the teeth reacted to the UV rays from the Blacklight.

2. The violet portion of the teeth is the vampire element of the teeth. Reasoning: The violet portion of the teeth altered when exposed to the UV rays. Human DNA would not have reacted to the UV rays, whether it was the white or violet part of the teeth.

Sunlight Questions

1. Could increased amounts of UV nanometers destroy the vampire teeth? If so, how would destruction take place?

2. Disinfection and decontamination of surfaces and water occurs between 240-280nm. Do UV rays in

this range, when they react with the vampire teeth, attempt to disinfect and decontaminate the teeth of the vampire element?

3. Medical light therapy and Bug "zappers" work in different UV nanometer ranges, respectively. Would either of these have an affect on the vampire teeth?

Test 7: Silver

Silver in European folklore has long been traditionally believed to be an antidote to fictional monsters. It was believed that a werewolf, in his bestial form, could only be killed by a weapon or bullet made of silver. There is a wide amount of disagreement on the affect of silver against vampires. Some believe silver to be a repellant against vampires because of the holy connotations of silver. Some also attribute vampire's dislike of silver to mirrors, which were originally polished silver. There are also those who believe that silver will not have any affect on a vampire, that silver is reserved only for the destruction of werewolves.

The scientist is inclined to believe there is some connection between silver and vampires because the vampire teeth were shipped in a silver container. The scientist did not experience any resistance from the teeth near the metal when removing or returning the teeth from the case, so he did not include the case in the earlier resistance tests. Silver, by itself, is not strong enough to be of general use. It is typically combined with copper as a strengthening agent. Perhaps the copper in the eyeglass case is enough to neutralize the affect of the silver on the vampire teeth? With this question in mind, the scientist went about conducting an acid test on the silver eyeglass case. The acid spot turned green, indicating the eyeglass case had a millesimal fineness of 500, meaning the eyeglass case was only 50% silver.

A question that has always troubled the scientist about the silver lore concerns other precious metals. Why is silver the metal of choice when repelling vampires? Why not gold, or copper, or gems such as emeralds or diamonds? Another item that the scientist wondered about concerning vampires was salt. Salt is documented in the Bible as a significant element in many stories, and the experiments concerning religious items delivered noticeable results, so logically salt could have an affect on vampires, yet it does not have the mythological connection silver does. Side note: When the scientist researched salt in connection with vampires on the

Internet, the majority of what appeared were references to a creature from an episode of one of the original Star Trek television shows.

There is also the concern on how to proceed with experiments with the teeth concerning silver. Minus the sunlight tests, the experiments thus far have focused on vampire repellants, with the sunlight tests being adjustable as not to injure or damage the teeth. All of the stories concerning silver and vampires tell of silver harming and burning vampires, although not killing them, as wooden stakes in the heart allegedly do.

Silver can be obtained that consists of various purity ranges, but that still does not remedy the fact that the teeth will have to be exposed to silver and observed for possible damages. (Side note: As well as observing and documenting the affects of silver on the vampire teeth, the scientist will also have the opportunity to observe and document possible regeneration, another common vampire lore.)

From a medical perspective, silver fillings have been used

for years in dental applications (as has gold). Therefore, if any results occur from the interaction of silver and the vampire teeth, the results will be from the silver interacting with the vampire component of the vampire teeth, not the human element.

The scientist debated on how to proceed with the silver tests. All of the remaining experiment categories were designed to test the truculent nature of various vampire lore, thus each additional experiment in each category may damage the teeth. With this in mind, the scientist elected to proceed with exposing the teeth to silver, deciding to proceed with the more aggressive tests than expand into greater detail with repellant tests.

The silver experiments will begin with Sterling silver. Sterling silver has a millesimal fineness of 925, meaning the silver alloy is 92.5% pure silver and 7.5 per cent copper or other metals. Once conclusions from the Sterling silver experiments can be derived, the scientist will then increase or decrease the silver ratio, per the results of the test. Side note:

As that the eyeglass case did not appear to affect the vampire teeth, the scientist does not see the purpose of testing silver on the teeth.

Silver: Test 1

One vampire tooth was touched by a 1mm square silver shaving. (A pair of tweezers held the silver shaving as it would have been too small to be hand held.) The first silver combination tested was Sterling silver.

Upon contact with the silver, the tooth began to sizzle with a slight vapor coming from the contact point. (The silver was in contact with the tooth for one second.) The scientist removed the silver to discover:

1) The corner area of the silver that had touched the vampire tooth was noticeably altered. Where the entire shaving was once a silver color, the area that had touched the tooth was now black. Upon review of the shaving under a microscope, the scientist was able to observe that the texture of the silver shaving

area had also altered, appearing similar to charred wood.

2) The vampire tooth now had a line in it where the shaving had touched it. The mark was comparable to the size of the area that the silver shaving had touched the tooth. The line was black in color, but thin, as if a fine point pencil had drawn the line.

Rather than continue testing the various silver qualities on the teeth, the scientist elected to pause the silver experiments to observe and document any possible regeneration from the vampire tooth. (Side note: vampire regeneration/immunization is a category the scientist will delve into in greater detail later in the journal.) After three days of observations, the teeth did not show any signs or indications of regeneration.

Silver: Test 2

The second silver test repeated the actions of the first

silver test, the planned variable being one vampire tooth was touched by a 1mm square Coin silver shaving this time. (Coin silver is 90% silver.) This time, however, the tooth did not appear to have any reaction to the silver. The scientist attempted the test with the second vampire tooth, believing that perhaps there was an unknown chemical alteration to the first tooth that was exposed to the higher quality silver. The second tooth did not appear to have any affect from the coin silver either.

Silver Conclusions

1. Silver can damage a vampire.
2. The amount of pure silver a vampire is exposed to is important in determining the affect of the silver on a vampire.

Silver Theories

1. Vampires cannot regenerate wounds caused by silver.
2. Sterling silver (92.5%) is strong enough to cause harm to vampires. Silver qualities under 90% do not appear to

cause harm.

Silver Questions

1. If they wanted to, could vampires apply a medicinal cure to silver wounds? If so, what would the treatment be?

2. Antique crosses made of Sterling silver are common. What would be the affect be if a vampire were touched by one of these crosses, since the silver cross combines two different components vampires object to?

Test 8: Blood

The final experiments of this study focused on how vampire teeth respond to blood. For safety concerns, the scientist had purposely postponed these experiments to the end of the study. Side note: there were too many variables and too much unknown data to fulfill these tests prior to the other tests of the study.

Each animal species has a unique blood type. There are

similarities between the types, and it is unknown how significant the alterations between the types are to vampires, or if the variables matter to them at all.

The temperature of the blood is an area these tests will investigate. Vampires are infamous for attacking humans and other animals to drink the blood of their victim.

A common lore within the vampire world is a vampire cannot drink the blood of the dead. These beliefs will be tested in the following experiments.

Scientific facts about blood:

1. Plasma, red blood cells (erythrocytes), white blood cells (leukocytes), and thromobocytes (platelets) are the core components of blood.

2. Blood is 90% water.

3. The other 10% consists of proteins (albumin, fibrinogen, and globulins), nutrients (glucose, fatty acids, amino acids), waste products (urea, uric acid, lactic acid, creatinine), clotting factors, minerals, immunoglobulins, hormones, and carbon dioxide.

4. The amount of blood in the human body depends on size (body mass is more important than height). An average man of 150 lbs or 70 kgs will have around 8 pints or 5.2 liters of blood. A woman of 110 lbs (50 kgs) will have about 3.3 liters of blood; about 5 pints.

5. The average blood transfusion consists of 3 pints.

Blood: Test One

1. The blood from a cow was purchased from a local butcher. The blood was neither warmed nor cooled from the temperature from when it was obtained from the butcher.

2. The blood was collected and stored in a small Petri dish (60mmx15mm).

3. A 3 ml disposable plastic eyedropper collected a full 3ml of blood from the Petri dish.

4. A vampire tooth was removed from the eyeglass

case.

5. A drop of cow's blood was dropped onto the vampire tooth.

6. The cow's blood rolled off the tooth. No response recognized.

   a. Possible reasons for no response:

      i. The blood must be fresh from the body of the donor for a vampire to be satisfied.

      ii. Both teeth must be present for there to be reaction to blood.

      iii. A biological element from a vampire must be present for a reaction/response to occur.

Possible Reason II was tested when both teeth were combined in the glass box with the cow's blood placed on them. Once again, no reaction nor response observed.

This data allowed the scientist to hypothesize a reason for the lack of response from the vampire teeth during the cow's blood test to be either possible reason #1, #3, or another reason that could not be formulated with the data collected thus far in the experiments.

(The scientist elected to pursue testing possible reason #1 as that possible reason #3 would require a live vampire to experiment with.)

Blood: Test Two

1. The blood from a "feeder" mouse was obtained from a mouse purchased at a pet store.
2. The blood was collected and stored in a small petri dish (60mmx15mm).
3. A 3 ml disposable plastic eyedropper collected a full 3ml of blood from the Petri dish.
4. A vampire tooth was removed from the eyeglass case.
5. A drop of mouse's blood was dropped onto the vampire tooth.
6. The vampire's tooth absorbed the mouse's blood. The vampire tooth's veins, which had been purple in appearance, had changed color to a purple-pink hue.

7. The scientist dropped another drop of the mouse's blood on the tooth. Once again, the vampire tooth absorbed the blood drop. The color of the vein's in the tooth changed color again, this time to a softer pink color.

8. The scientist conducted the same experiment again with the mouse's blood with a third drop of blood. The same sequence of events occurred, this time with the veins in the tooth completely disappearing from view. (The second vampire tooth was inspected; it still maintained the purple veins the other tooth had displayed at the beginning of the tests.

Side Note: The rough area that was created during the Holy water test and the pencil thin mark that was created during the silver test lessened in intensity after each drop of the mouse's blood was applied. After the third drop of blood was administered, both the roughness and the mark had been removed, the tooth appearing to have returned to the state it was in at the beginning of the experiments.

Blood Conclusions

1. The vampire teeth do react to blood.

2. Vampire teeth can differentiate between different kinds of   blood.

3. Not all blood will produce a reaction with the vampire teeth.

4. When the teeth are exposed to blood, the teeth react to the blood.

Blood Questions

1. What about blood are vampires attracted to?

2. How much blood does a vampire need to ingest?

3. Can a vampire tell the difference between blood types?

4. Does blood temperature matter?

5. Will plasma work in place of blood?

Blood Theories

1. The freshness of the blood is relevant when the
    vampire teeth are exposed to blood.

2. There is an unknown element/molecule in fresh blood
    that creates the reaction the vampire teeth illustrated
    during the tests.

3. It will require the study of a complete vampire to
    deduce what the unknown element/molecule is that
    create the blood reaction.

Appendix 1: Holy Water Acquisition

(As this is a story of what took place, I elected to write
this in first person to communicate more of the
emotions I felt during this escapade.)

Islam in Romania is followed by only 0.3 percent of
population, but has 700 years of tradition in Northern
Dobruja, a region on the Black Sea coast, which was

part of the Ottoman Empire for almost five centuries (ca. 1420-1878.) Ninety-seven percent of the Romanian Muslims are residents of the two counties forming Northern Dobruja: eighty-five percent live in Constanța County, and twelve percent in Tulcea County. Most of Romania's Muslims are Sunnis. As of this writing, there are 35 Imams (clergy) in Romania.

I considered leaving Romania to go to a country that was richer with Islamic clergy. However, it was more practical to exhaust my chances of acquiring Islamic Holy Water while in Romania before extending my travel area.

(Without divulging the primary area where I was conducting my research, I will simply state I was far away from the coastal counties of Constanta and Tulcea.)

I rented a safe deposit box from a local bank to store the eyeglass case with the vampire teeth. This seemed a logical place to keep the teeth, thinking that if vampires could feel the essence of the teeth through the silver case AND the steel box, they would still have to penetrate the safe to acquire the teeth; an unlikely event, but still possible.

After putting the teeth in the deposit box, I went to the train station to travel to Constanta. The train stations in Romania are uniquely designed, merging elements of old railroad travel with modern technological requirements. I liked the comparison a friend of mine once said about such things: "Tron meets Butch Cassidy."

Between changing trains, the atypical rail delays, and just the travel alone, it would take many hours to reach Constanta. I looked forward to the time away from my work. I enjoyed what I was doing, but it was also very intense work, and very lonely work as well. I dared not to communicate with anyone via computer for fear they could track my signal and locate his general proximity of my traveling laboratory.

Constanta was always a place I had wanted to visit. The Genoese Lighthouse was on top of the reasons. A sculpted lighthouse sounded amazing. There was also the House with Lions and other buildings that were famous for their architecture and beauty. I found it ironic that, due to the reason for my trip to Constanta, one of the most famous building *in* Constanta was the Great Mahmudiye Mosque. Would holy water derived from significant holy places deliver greater sanctity in my experiments? This is something I would keep in mind for future tests; this set of tests just needs to confirm basic information.

I did not realize how mentally exhausted I was until I got on the train. As soon as I sat down in one of the chairs, I felt as if this enormous weight was off my shoulders. I looked around at some of the other people on the train. A young couple with backpacks appeared to be nature tourists. There was a woman with a child in her lap that was flipping through a book. I was semi-jealous of all of them as they lived what appeared normal lives. With what I knew and the research I was conducting, I was as far away from normal as one could probably get without going insane.

Yet at the same time, I was happy for them. I was happy that they did not have any clue of the world I was delicately dancing in. In a sense, it felt good to know I was doing something for these people, in the event they ever needed my research. In another sense, it felt good to know there was a world outside of the disturbing world of vampires, and people were thriving in it.

I closed my eyes for a moment, but quickly fell asleep. I dreamt of being back in America, seeing my family. I had not seen them in a few years, but that was of my own choosing, my own mistakes. It took learning of the underworld to pull me out of my own abyss and I realized the poetry of the situation; I had traded my own abyss for another. Yet in this one, I had a purpose, a reason for living, a cause to fight for. The other was my own self-pity, my own selfishness. As odd as this may sound, I much preferred the world of vampires compared to my own world of addictions.

I woke up about 15 minutes before the train stopped at the station I was supposed to switch trains at. I took a bottle of water out of my bag and took a drink, the water feeling good against my throat from sucking in the stale air of the train compartment. For a moment, I wondered if this was how blood felt against a vampire's throat that hadn't eaten in some time. Then I realized how much I was looking at things in the vampire world compared to my own. Wasn't sure how I felt about that....

It was going to be about an hour before my next train. (When traveling by train, everything is about since nothing is ever even close to being on time.) There was little cafe within walking distance to the station where I could hear if when the train was pulling in, so I elected to go there and get a cup of coffee and maybe something to eat.

The Fox Cafe was a quaint little place, the type of place you would associate with traveling in Europe. There was a bar area against the main window where people could look out towards the train station. (Apparently, I was not the first to come to the Fox for coffee while awaiting a train.) I went to counter and ordered a large mocha. The person asked if I would like

Austrian chocolate in my mocha instead of the regular kind. I said sure; I was still American enough to grab anything European when it was offered since it was only a few days away the country where it was produced.

I took my coffee over to the bar by the window. There was a girl there with iPod headsets in her ears. She wasn't bad looking, and she scooted her stool over some once she saw me sitting near her. I smiled and put my hand up as if to signal I had enough room. She smiled back and nodded. I pointed to my ear, then I pointed to her ears, trying once again to signal a question about what she was listening to.

She opened her mouth as if to say "Ah", but nothing was said. She pulled one of her earpods from her ear and said in perfect British English "Yes." I responded quickly with a smile on my face. "You're from England?!"

"Yes, and you're a Yank!" She appeared to be just as excited to find someone who spoke English in rural Romania as I was.

"So, what part of England are you from?" I inquired.

"London. Islington area. And you?"

"My folks used to live in Massachusetts, but now they live down in Florida."

"Oh really? Been to Disneyworld, have you?" I

couldn't tell if she was sincere or joking from her question. I thought I'd play it safe with my reply.

"No. No Disneyworld for me. I've been over here for the past few years. How about you?"

The girl pointed to the train station. "I am heading up to Brasov on the next train. You ever been to Brasov?"

All of a sudden, this felt like a dream. Brasov was where I had found out about the vampires, went through chemical dependency treatment, done my first round of teeth testing, and met vampires for the first time. "Yes," I said, "I have been to Brasov."

The girl became enthusiastic about hearing about Brasov, wanting to know the things worth seeing and the things that were over-rated. I tried to describe Brasov without sounding too much like a tourist guide, but at the same time not wanting to disillusion her to what was, and probably still was, a beautiful city.

She asked "Is there any place I should go that most people don't know about?"

I thought about the Diamond Cafe, the place where I used to hang out with my friend Yuri Donsky. Yuri was the one who educated me about vampires while we were roommates, and I had to sacrifice that friendship for me to pursue my scientific research. "Go to a place called the Diamond Cafe. It is a quaint little coffeehouse with lots of pretty oak woodwork. Not too hard to find, and the prices are reasonable." In my heart, I wish I could have gone with her. For a moment, I fantasized about traveling on a train with a pretty girl back to my old stomping grounds.

As if she saw me thinking this, she asked, "Where are you going?" I informed her that I, too, was traveling by train, but I was headed for Constanta.

She smiled brightly and replied, "I'm just coming from there! It's an amazing place! You ever been there before?" I told her I had not, and then she continued.

"Oh, you gotta check out the House of Lions, and the casino, even if you don't gamble. And the Hunchiar mosque, and the first Carol mosque. I'm not Muslim or anything, but those building are just cool as school to look at!"

I chucked at her excitement, as well as her innocence. There was no way she could have known why I was going to Constanta, or what I needed to do there, yet she was advising me on which mosques to go to. I had already known about these mosques, but I found her talking about them incredibly serendipitous.

I put my hand up to gesture her to stop. "Before you on, I don't even know your name?"

She rolled her eyes backwards in an "I'm so stupid" action before answering. "My name is Felicity. And yours?"

Before asking her name, I had decided giving her my real name wouldn't endanger her or me. She was tourist after all and still in the fog with everyone else where it came to vampires. I stuck my hand out to invite a handshake. "Steve."

She grabbed my hand and shook it. "Pleased to meet you, Steve the Yank."

I retorted "You as well, Felicity from Islington."

Felicity spoke again. "So are you on Facebook? I'd love to talk to you more about your trip and see your pictures!"

Oh boy. Now I'm into it.

"I don't have a Facebook account. I had a situation where things got ugly so I got rid of it." Ugly being every vampire and Catholic fanatic on the planet was looking for me.

"Oh bummer! Well, you can look at mine. Felicity Rapp. Islington."

I replied in a flirtatious manner "Oh, here I was hoping you were going to tell me your name was Felicity Shagwell, like in those Austin Powers movies."

Felicity slapped my chest. "Oh Steve, behave!" Her quote from the movie with her British accent sure was a turn on!

Felicity and I spent the next hour chitchatting about a

Vampirology

variety of things. She let me listen to her music, which she titled "progressive heavy metal." I liked it, kind of like Yes meets Metallica. Her train came in before mine, and I walked her over to the station. She referred to one of my favorite films, *Before Sunrise,* the plot of which is two people meet at a train station overnight while waiting for two different trains. A small romance emerges, and they agree to meet one year to the day at the same station again. Felicity and I did not agree to such a meeting, but I did mention I may try to engage her on Facebook.

My train was not long after Felicity's, so I just stayed at the station and drank the coffee I had gotten to go from the cafe. As I sat there, I wondered if I was ever going to have a "normal" life ever again. Now I know there is no such thing as a "normal" life, but I'd say 99.5% of the population lives in a world without vampires. I am in the .5% that has them, and I just wondered if I would ever be in a position with what I am doing where I could I have a girlfriend, a family, etc.

Even though I had an ample amount of coffee while talking to Felicity, I fell asleep on the train again. It felt really good to just sit there and do.....nothing. Furthermore, on this trip, no one was around me. If you haven't traveled in a foreign land, you may not understand how nice it is to be somewhere where people aren't talking in their local dialect; it is very easy for your brain to get convoluted around deciphering the words, even if you aren't part of the conversation. Romania had so many different languages it was easy to get lost in translations, and it was really nice to sit on the train and just have the sounds of traveling in my ears.

It was a restful sleep. No dire dreams about anything. I woke up slightly groggy, a sign to me just how deep into sleep I really was. Once again, I woke up 15 minutes before the train pulled into the station. (As a scientist, I would have liked to know why I had this synchronicity of waking when I needed to.) I got off the train and immediately smelled the slightest hint of the sea. I closed my eyes and breathed in the air again, the salty air so pleasant to smell after being inland for such a long time.

I would have preferred to wander around and take in some of the atmosphere, but it was turning dusk and a shower at the hotel sounded great too. I hailed a cab to take me to the Hotel Maria.

After a shower and a change of clothes, I decided to

go out and get something to eat down by the seashore. I was really hoping to find some place that had a "catch of the day" since we were right by the Caspian Sea. The hotel was only a few blocks away from the water, and I was able to find a nice place after only a few minutes.

The Konak reminded me of some of the restaurants I used to go to back in New York. The signage was bold and in dark red, accented by stainless steel. The front entry had the door open, and smells of spices came wafting into my nose, just like the aromas of the restaurants and cafes back in New York. Although I couldn't know for sure, it had the appearance of being a family owned restaurant, one that had been started generations ago.

I entered the restaurant to find they did indeed have a fresh catch from this morning: red mullet. The waitress told me "There is nothing better than a crispy, salty and perfectly cooked red mullet. It can be tricky to get it just right and out chef is very good at it." With an endorsement like that, I felt mandated to order it.

As I waited for my salad, I looked around the room. In many ways, I felt as if I had stepped into a time warp. There was music being played...by actual musicians! There weren't any televisions either, at least none I could see.

V a m p i r o l o g y

It felt odd being at such a nice restaurant without a date. It would have been nice to have Felicity here, but by now, she was probably in Brasov. Heck, for all I knew, she was at the Diamond Cafe updating her Facebook page. I was sure I was going to enjoy my dinner, but if I had my choice, I'd be in Brasov.

Eventually, my salad and meal arrived. The salad was heavy with feta cheese and olives. The red mullet arrived as "whole fish"; the entire fish was cooked and was looking at me through crispy breading. Once I got used to the appearance of my meal, I began to eat it, and it was delicious!

I declined a desert, although I was very tempted.

I left the Konak and went for a walk along the seaboard. They had a sidewalk area next to the seawall with ample amount of lighting. In many ways, it reminded me of a rustic version of Atlantic City. There were some shops open, but I didn't go in them. Instead, I went and read about the sea and the sea wall at a large placard that had a bunch of information on it. As I was reading, a man came up on my right to read the sign too. He appeared to be close to my height, black haired, wearing a nice leather coat.

"There is a lot of information to absorb in one reading, yes?" The waves were crashing against the wall, and even though he was about arm's distance from me, I could still hear him when he spoke. He had an accent, but it did not sound European nor Middle Eastern.

I replied. "Too much for me to grasp."

He spoke again. "You are an American. You are here to study the sea?" He waved towards the dark water in front of us.

I smiled at this, thinking if this man really knew what I was studying, the sea would be hell bent and gone in comparison. "No, just a tourist."

The stranger smiled at this and spoke. "A tourist? In Romania? You must be here for the vampires then?"

I shook my head. "No. Just here to enjoy Constanta and the sea."

The stranger came closer to me and said. "Oh, but I think you are." Then turned and walked back towards the buildings.

Oh shit.

I turned around to see the stranger standing 10' from me, his body turned slightly toward the buildings, but not enough for his back to me. He stood there in a slight silhouette; an ominous sign considering what he had just said to me. He waved at me to join him. I

Vampirology

hesitated, wondering what I was getting myself into. If this guy was a vampire, he could attack me at any minute. Yet if he wanted to attack me, why would he be waving for me to come with him into a more populated, better lit environment?

He motioned again for me to join him. I chose to go towards the light and people. I could decide as we walked if I wanted to continue to engage in a conversation with this person, since I was not sure yet if he was a vampire.

When I was 5' from the man, he turned away from the sea and started walking towards the buildings. When I caught up to him I asked "What did you mean back there?"

The man smiled and continued walking. "Let's go get something to drink, or better yet, something to eat. Have you had dinner yet?" I told the stranger I had just finished dining when I arrived at the placard and that I didn't drink.

"Not even coffee?" He inquired.

"No, I drink coffee."

"Then let's go get a cup of coffee." I was confused by his series of statements. It was still too dark for me to see if there were any signs of this man being a vampire, so I had to rely on my instincts. A coffee-drinking vampire did not make sense, and I was still enticed by his earlier statement, so I agreed to get a cup of coffee with him.

He led us towards a small little place called the Seaside Cafe. The interior was decorated with an assortment of seaside things and ship items. Driftwood, seashells, and glass floats; not the type of place a person envisions when pondering if they are going to be attacked by a vampire.

The man went and took a seat in a booth towards the rear of the cafe. I think I would have really liked the place, if I hadn't had been brought here under such odd circumstances. I sat across from the stranger in the burgundy-padded booth. It was brighter in the cafe, but the light we were under had a yellow glass dome, so it was still hard to ascertain the paleness of the man.

A waitress came and took our order. "Get whatever you like," I was instructed. "I will pay the bill." I ordered a small coconut latte. The stranger, however, did not order anything. Now I was worried.

The waitress left and I didn't say anything. I was apprehensive to tip my hand in this poker game that just walked up to me five minutes ago. The stranger smiled and as if he was reading my mind said "Do not worry. I am not going to attack you." Well, that settled whether he was a vampire or not.

The stranger stretched his arm over the back of the

booth. "Now you are wondering why I approached you on the walkway outside." I still did not speak. "Does the cat have your tongue? You can speak to me in any language you like; I am fluent in many."

I opened my mouth, but did not say anything. I considered talking in Latin or some obscure language to test his statement, but thought better of it. No, this was a time to be conservative. Thank goodness, the waitress arrived with my coffee and broke the tension.

I took a drink of my coffee. The stranger asked "It is to your liking?" I nodded that it was. "Don't worry about me; I'll have something later." I shot back against the booth, looking at him startled. The stranger smiled back at me. "It comes with the territory. You have to have what you need. I....I have to have what I need."

The stranger repositioned himself in the booth. "What is your name? Since we are discussing such delicate matters, I do believe it to be good form to know each other, yes? I am Omar. And you?"

"My name is Cale." I said this pseudonym in a very deadpan tone.

"I doubt if that is your real name, but it will suffice for now. You....you are an odd one, Mr. Cale. You are not a vampire, nor are you a lackey to one either. Yet, you have an essence about you that I could not ignore when I was walking outside."

Now this was new. I had been working with the vampire teeth behind the protective plastic shields of the glove box. To hear that I was carrying a vampire essence from being exposed to the teeth...this was amazing. I also felt disappointed in myself for not thinking about the spiritual safety factors of the teeth. I had gone to great efforts in the realm of the physical, but had not done anything for spiritual safety. Nor had I been cleansed through a clergy person of any faith. Well, too late for that now.

"I don't know what you are talking about." In a sense, I didn't, either.

Omar squinted at me. "Vampires have increased senses to detect things. One of these is the ability to "sense" when a vampire is near, or, in your case, a human who has dealings with vampires. You, however, Mr. Cale, do not have the typical essence of a vampire servant. Actually, I have never sensed the essence I feel with you, and I am, as you Americans say, long in the tooth."

Great. Not only am I having coffee with a vampire, but a vampire comedian.

Omar continued. "So, Mr. Cale, I will ask you, what do you do in the vampire world?" Omar sat and looked at me, not blinking, not moving. Was he trying to hypnotize me? Was he using his increased senses to get another kind of reading from me? I couldn't tell, and that sounded like a good answer to give him.

I replied in the same deadpan tone I delivered my name with. "I can't talk about it."

"Cannot, or will not?" Omar asked.

"Both" I answered.

Omar looked around the cafe, then came back to look upon me. "I am here as a pilgrim. A follower returning to the Holy Land, if you would. I had never been to Romania before. I have been here only a day now, and I run into you. I know nothing about you or why you are the way you are, and I have yet to meet any other vampires to talk to about you, so I will have to let your answer suffice for now. But I will tell you, Mr. Cale, I have been the way I am for a very long time, and after such a long time, new things rarely develop, and you are a new thing. This is something we will re-visit."

"So am I safe from attack until you and the other vampires get me figured out?" I knew my vampire-clock was ticking, and I wanted some sort of assurance that I would have some time to figure out how to get out of this mess.

Omar smiled. "In the vampire world, it is bad form to attack another vampire's lackey. In your world, it would be equivalent of you attacking another person's pet. Just not good manners. So you are safe, from me anyway, until I get some answers about you. Then, based on what I learn, I will make my decision on what to do with you."

Now I was really concerned. "To do with me?"

Omar smiled. "A human with too much vampire knowledge is dangerous to my kind. I may have to liquidate you on the basis of vampire self-preservation. But like I said, that all depends on what I learn from the other vampires here in Romania. There are vampires in Romania, yes?"

I knew what he was going to find out, and the next thought hit me:

Dammit! Dammit! Dammit! Dammit! Dammit!

After we were done, Omar went his way and I went mine. I thought about going back for a walk on the seaside, but after spending the better part of an hour with a vampire, I really wanted to be around people, so I went back into the downtown area. The smell of the sea made me question my own aromas in the world of the undead. I wondered if there were any other vampires getting a drift of my "essence". I also felt like every person whom I came into eye contact with was analyzing me, and that, combined with the chat I had with Omar, was enough to make me take some quick actions.

Before going back to my hotel, I stopped off at a small market and bought garlic cloves and a cross. (I never thought I would be having to use my research for my own benefit, but I was glad I knew it!) I deduced that the combination of these two things, plus Omar's lukewarm insurance of not being attacked for a few days would provide me at least one night of safety while I try to come up with some sort of plan to save my ass.

It was odd walking through the lobby of a four-star hotel with a bag full of vampire deterrents. The objects were in a paper bag, but even with what I knew, I still felt a little silly. I had requested a room above the 10th floor as so I could look out at the sea, I didn't realize I would be using it for my own protection. (There were vampire stories that vampires could fly, but while I was writing the possible tests I could perform on the vampire teeth, I wasn't able to formulate a test to see if they could. At this point, I was hoping that their ability to fly was just a myth.)

There is also the myth that a vampire cannot enter a room unless they are invited. However, this is a hotel room. In the vampire world, would my renting this room constitute ownership? I wasn't going to take any chances. I called the front desk and left firm instructions that I did not want to be disturbed no matter who asked for me at the front desk.

I placed a garlic clove at each corner of the window and door. I placed the cross by my bed, and proceeded to prepare for bed like any other night, except this place was head and shoulders greater than my standard laboratory lodgings (like hot water, no rats, etc.) The one thing that did cross my mind was how much I could appreciate a good, stiff drink. The problem with me was one good stiff drink would lead to two, then three, then four.....you get the picture.

I thought about sleeping in the bathroom to add another layer of protection. It was decadent enough to serve as a bathroom; dark wood paneling with white marble fixtures with glass doors instead of a shower curtain. Although the idea of sleeping under a sunlamp was attractive, I decided against it. When I was drinking and using, I spent many a night in bathrooms, albeit not as posh as this one. I heard myself say "I'll be damned if I was going to go back to sleeping in one because of vampires. Let the bastards come and get me, at least I'd go out with some pride!"

I hopped into bed and turned on the TV. Life is full of little ironies and twists: the TV show that came on was a travel Romania show that was focusing on, you guessed it, Transylvania. I rolled my eyes and turned off the TV.

I had left a few lights on so I could see if anything, or anyone, was in the room during the night. It created a somber atmosphere, so I took advantage of the setting and started meditating about my situation. Should I change hotels after tonight? I could, but if I still had this vampire essence that Omar discovered, what good would it do to move? No, the better thing to do would be to go to a church tomorrow and get cleansed, blessed, sanctified, and spiritually scrubbed as much as possible.

But then a thought occurred to me: what if I get rid of this essence and Omar finds me again? The essence will be gone. I would just be a regular human being again. He might try to attack me at that time just to eradicate me and my confusing nature to the him and the vampire world.

I considered this for some time, then elected to go the sanctification route. By the time Omar did find me in a cleansed state, he probably would have talked to other vampires, and they would have told him there was a human scientist doing tests on vampire teeth. Once he learned this information, it would be logical for him to deduce that he had met the scientist, be upset that he had not destroyed me when he had the chance, and be eager to rectify his mistake. Without the vampire essence, I would be harder to locate.

There was also the desire within me to get rid of this essence. In the event the vampires did get me, I wanted to be purer spiritually than I was. I would like to think that whatever lies beyond would look at my life and see I was trying to be of use to mankind now rather than a self-motivated addict, but a little extra insurance of a good spiritual cleansing wouldn't hurt.

After finishing this round of thoughts, the smooth cool sheets of the bed took over and I fell asleep.

When I had called the front desk to leave my do not disturb direction, I also requested a wakeup call for 30 minutes before sunrise. I had to get myself cleansed and get the holy water before it turned dark again, so I had to make use of every second of daylight I could get before night, and the vampires, returned. I was still very sleepy when the phone call came. My body called for me to go back to sleep, and oh how I wanted too! I stayed in a limbo-esque state while I woke up, sucking up every piece of warm bedding I could. Then I felt the urge to pee, which I often thought was God's way of making sure people got out of bed in the morning.

After tending to my urological needs, I jumped in

V a m p i r o l o g y

the shower and prepared for my day. I could have stayed in the shower for much longer than I did. The combination of the heat lamp and the warm water were so wonderful words cannot describe it. I wanted to pack up this shower unit and take it back with me to my lab, even though I could only use it occasionally, with my constant moving. Still, it would have been worth it!

Even though the mosques were closer to the hotel, I elected to go get sanctified first. I didn't know about the Islamic faith and sanctification, so I decided I had better stick to what I knew, good old-fashioned Christianity. The front desk was able to point me in the direction of the closest Catholic Church.

I considered taking a cab, but I elected to walk instead, which I was glad I did. It was refreshing to be exercising so early in the morning. The downtown area was just starting to wake up as well, so there weren't copious amounts people or cars hustling about. The sun was rising over the Black Sea, and this made the reflective downtown buildings glisten. If not for the reason I was awake, this would have been a perfect moment.

The church the hotel had sent me to ended up being the cathedral of Constanta! A beautiful building that would have challenged Notre Dame for architectural significance, the stone appeared soft, probably from the sea air and sand hitting it over the centuries. I felt so humble climbing the steps of this magnificent church; it made me wonder if this was one of the motivations of the architects when they designed it.

A different thought came across me as I walked into the main archway. "I am Sir Steve of Yank, and I am here to be blessed before going into battle by the monks of Constanta. The Crusades you ask? No, I am off to fight a greater threat than the Persians or the Turks. A Dragon you ask? No, not a dragon. A dragon would be a tougher fight, but I would still be victorious. No, I am here to be blessed before I go up against the undead, for they are crossing the river Styx, and I alone possess the skills and knowledge to defeat the accursed that wish to slay us or convert us to their evil ways." I felt I should have been in a suit of armor with a steed waiting for me at the base of the steps. Note to self: create a coat of arms in my downtime at the laboratory.

Just one of the massive doors to the cathedral was propped open. The other wooden mass had an elaborate sign indicating the hours the cathedral was open, when confessions were, when mass was, etc. Interestingly, today was a holy day in the Catholic faith, so they cathedral was opened earlier than usual. I liked the idea of being blessed on a holy day, as if the

V a m p i r o l o g y

blessing on such a day would be a blessing on steroids... (Note to self...research if this is an actual belief. Perhaps holy water is stronger if it is sanctified on holy days?)

The special mass was to start in 20 minutes, so I went to the confessional, hoping I could be blessed before the mass started. As I said, I was not Catholic, and the idea of an extended mass in Romanian dialect did not sound very attractive to me, especially considering the tasks I had to address this day.

I tuned on the light to indicate I was in the confessional. As I sat there, I absorbed the atmosphere of the cubicle. Even though the light inside was dim, I could still see the ancient woodwork that could easily be over 100 years old. I considered all of the people who have sat in this spot, and I wondered over the years if any other people have sat here with vampire concerns. This was Romania after all, and although my situation was unique, I was not so closed-minded to think I was the only one ever to encounter the undead. The air in the cubicle had a smell of....purity. I wasn't sure if it was cleaning solutions or incense interacting with the salty sea air, but the aroma was soothing to my soul.

The door opened in the cubicle next to me and I heard the priest sit down. Didn't really see him, but I guess that's the way it is supposed to be. The priest settled in and then addressed me. His voice sounded older, but not elderly; male sounding, but not deep. I asked if the priest could speak English, and I was very glad when he answered yes.

I began talking. "I am not Catholic sir, but I am in a predicament that I sure would like a blessing or a prayer." I took a deep breath when I was done. It felt good to be able to talk to someone about this. Even though I was avoiding any details, it was nice to be in a place where I could let my guard down.

The priest replied in an accented, yet calm voice. "I see." Then there was a slight pause before he asked "Do you believe in God?" I took another extended breath before answering. I didn't really believe in the dogmas of any particular religion, but between recovering from my addictions and witnessing the effects of holy items on the vampire teeth, I was spiritually aware. I answered "Yes."

"Then the trouble you face is in this world, not the next, and with that, so many beautiful and wonderful tidings can be available to you, no matter what you are facing, my son." I took a moment to consider what the priest said. It was poetic, soothing, and relieving. The priest continued. "If you don't mind me asking, what are the problems you face?"

Oh boy. Another deep breath on my part. Could I talk to this man about vampires? He is clergy, and this is Romania, yet I was also reluctant. I decided the play it safe. "It is a complicated story Father. I'm.....in a tricky situation that could go bad real easy. I feel I am doing the right things for the right reasons, but that doesn't make what I have to do any easier."

"I see. So you believe what you are doing is of good motive?"

I felt my head nodding in agreement with this question. "Yes." Throughout everything that was going on, this was the one thing I still felt committed to, and I was willing to die for what I was doing.

The priest retorted to my answer. "In Scriptural language, to bless a person or thing signifies "to take a pleasure in it" or "to look upon it with approval." If you believe in our Holy Father, and you believe what you do is for the right reasons, I would like to encourage your struggle with a blessing." I heard the priest moving and saw his silhouette moving through the screen. I was rather numb when I heard "May the Lord bless you and keep you. May the Lord make his face to shine upon you, and be gracious to you. May the Lord lift up his countenance upon you, and give you peace."

When he was done, I asked if there was anything else he could do besides bless me. The priest replied

"A blessing is like full coverage insurance, my son. A blessing from God is all encompassing, even into things we did not think of when we received the blessing. That is how our Heavenly Father loves and cherishes his children." I liked that. I didn't know how well that was going to work against the vampires, but I liked it. Then I wondered how long the blessing would last, so I asked the priest this question "A blessing does not have an expiration date. If you stay true to the path of righteousness, then the blessing will help you stay the course. If you sin, it will help you stave off further pain and suffering." So there wasn't a definitive answer; guess I would have to live with that.

I thanked the priest and left the confessional. The mass was getting ready to start, so there were more people in the cathedral than when I went in. I put a few lieu (Romanian money) in the donation box and made my way to the exit. Before I left, I stopped and splashed some holy water on my face. Not much, mind you, but about the same amount one would use if it were after shave, which I thought about as I applied the water. I walked in with Essence of Vampire; I left with the Cologne of Divinity.

The downtown area was active now. More cars and buses were moving in the streets. I thought about walking around and seeing if anyone responded to my

"Spiritual updates," but then I remembered it was daytime and there wouldn't be any vampires awake to look for responses from in the first place. Even so, I felt refreshed, ready to tackle the day ahead of me.

For some odd reason, I was very hungry. I rarely ever ate breakfast, but this morning I was famished. There was a small restaurant across the street from the cathedral, so I went over to it to see what they had. The smell of coffee hit me as soon as I stepped onto the sidewalk near the open front door. A woman passed by me with a feta cheese Danish, and I was sold on one of those right then and there. I went in and got a cup of coffee and a few of those Danishes, which were as good as any I had ever had before. (As I recall this part of the story, my mouth is watering just thinking about them!)

I took my food and went back outside to sit and people watch. As a scientist, I was always keeping an eye open for things, but there was also part of me that enjoyed watching life take place. With my new vocation as a vampire scientist, I rarely had the opportunity to engage anyone, much less take the time to sit and be one with the public. This was indeed a rare occasion, and I enjoyed just being a regular person going through the everyday motions like anyone else in the world

Vampirology

might be doing as well.

The combination of the Danish, the coffee, and the blessing I received made me feel as if I could take on the world. When I was into my addiction, I often felt bulletproof, but this was different. That feeling was a chemically induced illusion; this was an emotional reality, and I much preferred this to the other. I rose from where I was sitting, tossed my garbage in the can nearby, and proceeded to walk in the direction of the Carol mosque.

The Carol Mosque is located in Ovid Square area of Constanta. It is the main religious Muslim edifice in Romania. The building started in 1910 at the initiative of King Carol I (after whom the building is named) and was completed in 1913. The main element that draws attention is a 47 meters high minaret that dominates the area; even though inland, it can be seen from the sea. (The Hunchiar mosque, the other mosque Felicity suggested I visit, was not a functioning mosque. It was damaged during World War II, so it is not used very much, just special occasions.)

Even though it was a nice day and I had my new aura about me, it felt odd strolling about downtown Constanta. I still felt that several people were looking at me, even though I knew the vampires were asleep and I had been sanctified by the priest. I also took into consideration my general addict paranoia, something that developed over years of looking over one's shoulder to make sure you aren't busted by the cops, beaten for your stash, etc.

I did see the humor of my life at that moment however. I had just left a Catholic cathedral and was now on my way to, arguably, the most famous mosque in Romania for their holy water. I laughed to myself as I thought, "What kind of messed up tourist am I?" This insight helped me get rid of my paranoia and return to enjoying the walk to the mosque.

I turned the corner and entered into the part of Constanta referred to as "Old Town". At the same time a sign appeared identifying this classic neighborhood, I caught my first glimpse of the tower. It was indeed an impressive sight, resembling something one might expect with a castle rather than a religious structure. The roads in this part of town were wedged very tightly between the buildings, probably a throwback to when horses and carts maneuvered through there. No sidewalks were available, so I had to dance and walk at the same time to avoid parked cars, delivery trucks, open store doors, and other assorted hazards.

I arrived at the main entry to the mosque. I had

expected a grand entryway, something parallel in magnificence to the tower and architecture seen from afar. But this was not the case. At the bottom of the tower was a rather simple entry composed of two swinging doors, one of which was propped open with a large stone. There were some potted trees and other greenery around the entry, and there were a set of windows above the doors cascading in size to form an attractive artistic element, but this entry was quaint and simple compared to the mammoth entry to the cathedral I was at earlier in the morning.

I was glad I had gone to the cathedral for cleansing before coming to the mosque. I felt pure of heart entering the shrine, and I enjoyed the thought of not having the vampire essence taint my being for my first exposure to the Islamic faith. Actually, I felt like an ambassador. Here I was, an American scientist who had just been sanctified by the Catholic Church, entering an Islamic mosque for discussion (and hopefully acquisition) of their holy water. A unique position for this ex-junkie to be in!

I was ignorant how I was going to proceed from this point. I had managed to get here, and I knew what I wanted, but as far as obtaining the water, I was clueless. It would have been convenient if there has been a stoup in the entryway as there was with Catholic churches, but that was not how things were here. Nor did I see any vases or bottles near the altar area. Then a thought occurred to me: maybe since the faith had developed over the centuries in the Middle East where water was scarce was the reason there were few water-based ceremonies or entities in Islam. Would make sense, but that didn't help me out now trying to locate some.

This meant I had to find someone to help me, and I was not looking forward to this. It would have been nice to have some place to sit down, but the interior of the mosque was an open area, constructed as so patrons could kneel towards Mecca when they congregated at the Mosque for prayers. The large, clean, shining white marble floor slabs were beautiful, but impractical, and it made me wonder about how elderly Muslims attended prayer times. In the Catholic Church, people had the option to use the kneelers in the pews or not; I wondered if the Islamic faith had developed a similar compassionate stance towards handicapped people also.

It didn't help that I was the only person whom I could see in the mosque. The Cathedral was bustling about with people as it was a holy day, here the very opposite. I was wearing soft-soled shoes, yet it seemed each one of my steps echoed throughout the mosque. I started walking slower and softer, which reduced the sounds of my footsteps, but made me feel as if I were lurching around the mosque, and the last thing I wanted was for someone to get the idea that this American tourist was sneaking about.

I decided to go back outside and regroup my thoughts. I was overwhelmed and out of my depth with where I was. I was hectic inside myself too, which has always been a bad place for me to be. I started walking towards the door, shoe noise be damned. As I neared the main entry, I saw two men walking into the mosque. The men were about the same height and build. One man appeared to be in his 50's, the other in his 20's. Both men were wearing dishdashas, the common clothing choice for Muslim men.

The two men stopped talking to each other when they noticed me coming out of the Mosque. Both appeared curious and concerned about who I was and what I was doing there, yet they were not confrontational. I stopped walking when they noticed me. I was not yet out of the Mosque, but a few feet still inside the entry, about the same location someone would be if opening the door to a visitor in the home. Yet here I was the visitor, and these men, who were obviously Muslim, were in the position I should have been in. This chance arrangement made me feel even more awkward then I already was feeling.

The elder man put his fingertips together in front of his chest, nodded his head and said, "As-Salaam-Alaikum," the Arabic greeting meaning "Peace be unto you," the standard salutation among Muslims. I knew what their words meant, but I did not know the way to reply to this. I put my hands together in a similar fashion and nodded, hoping these gestures would communicate respect for them and their religion. I then spoke in Romanian. "Good morning. I was looking for the Imam and could not find anyone. Might either of you be him?" Both men smiled and nodded. The elder man spoke again, this time in Romanian. "We are the Imam for this Mosque. How may we help you?"

I breathed a sigh of relief and smiled. "Is there a place where we can sit and talk?" The elder man waved his hand towards the cement entryway to the Mosque and said "here." The man then talked to the other person he was with, who then walked away, returning with rugs for us to sit on the ground with. I was somewhat surprised by this, but then reconsidered where I was and the culture I was interacting with, and this made some sense.

The Imam sat first, and then directed me as to where I should place my rug. We faced each other across the walkway, neither of us with our backs to the road or the mosque. I wondered if he had done this many times before and knew that no one likes having their back to possible dangers. I sat down on the brown rug, which was more like a big terrycloth towel than a rug. Still, I was startled to find how comfortable it was.

After I positioned myself on the rug, I began talking. "Imam, I am very ignorant to your religion and way of life. I have questions that maybe you can help me answer?"

The Imam nodded. "Of course. What would you like to know about?"

"Abi Shifa water. It is holy water in your faith, yes?"

The Imam straightened his back, blinked a few times, and licked his lips. "Well now, this is something I did not expect to be talking about this morning." He had a slight smile on his face as he considered what to say next. "The first thing is I am a Sunni, and what you talk of is Shia, not Sunni. Do you understand the difference?"

I nodded. "Somewhat. The best I can explain is it is similar to the Christian faith having both Catholic and Protestants. Very similar in many things, but significant differences are still present."

The Imam wobbled his head a bit. "For the purposes of our conversation, those comparisons will work. However, since you have come here seeking information, and I know here in Romania Sunnis are the majority of the Muslims, I will try to represent the Shia ideals the best I can. But by no means am I an expert!" The Imam chuckled while he said this last sentence, which made me feel a bit more relaxed.

The Imam continued. "In the Shia faith, Karbala is a place where Shia mourn the death of Hazrat Ali, or as the western world call him, Ali.
While Sunnis consider Ali the fourth and final of the Rashidun caliphs, Shias regard Ali as the *first* Imam after Muhammad." The Imam took a moment to see if what he was saying was making any sense to me, which it was.

The Imam continued, moving his hands in subtle gestures along the way much like a good storyteller would. "All of this is due to the Shia's interpretation of the events at Ghadir Khumm. It was at Ghadir Khumm Shias maintain that in this hadith the Islamic prophet Muhammad appointed Ali as his heir and successor. The Sunnis, on the other hand, do not deny Muhammad's declaration about Ali at Ghadir Khumm, but they argue that he was simply urging the audience to hold his cousin and son-in-law in high esteem and affection This disagreement splits the Muslim community into the Sunni and Shia branches." The Imam stopped speaking, his hands open as if he were holding each belief in each hand.

After a slight pause, the Imam asked, "Would you like some water to drink?" I replied "Oh, no thanks. I'm good." I then proceeded to take a bottle of water from my bag. The Imam pulled a water bottle from his bag as well. I pointed to his water bottle. "It appears we drink the same brand." He smiled, understanding the slight joke I told.

After drinking the water, the Imam continued. "Now then, Abi Shifa in Persian means "healing water." Shias take a little bit of dust from Karbala and mix it with water, then drink it, believing that the dust from the sacred site will create Abi Shifa, healing water."

I repositioned myself on the rug. "And the Sunnis do not have such a water?" The Imam shook his head no. "We do not have the same connection with Karbala as the Shia."

Now I decided to go for the big question. "So how does one obtain Abi Shifa water?"

The Imams face and attitude changed. "Why do you want to know?"

Oh crap. I had been struggling with a rational way to address this question if were to be asked, and I never really did get a hold of a good answer.

I took my time answering. "Sir, you are a noble man, and I am afraid if I told you the truth, the *real* reason I wanted it, you would think me a fool or a lunatic. I could lie and formulate some sort of story, but I respect you and your faith too much to do that." I knew that I was risking not having the Imam's help with obtaining the Abi Shifa water by saying this, but it also felt good being totally honest. After all, this was a Sunni man, and I could still get some Abi Shifa water somewhere else, albeit I did not have a clue how to or where to start.

The Imam sat silently and considered what I said. He considered it for a longer time than I would have preferred, and his silence made me wonder if I should be saying more, but I chose not to. There is truth in that old saying "Less is more."

After a few minutes, the Imam spoke in a somber tone. "I am honored that you did not lie to me. Whatever pains your life right now must be serious, yet I am also concerned when people cannot divulge details. I am a Muslim in a Christian country, and I grew up in a Communist Romania. I wouldn't go so far to say I am a paranoid person, just extra careful about things. You have been honest with me, but you haven't told me the entire truth, either."

I closed my eyes and nodded in agreement, appreciating what the Imam had said. I opened my eyes and spoke to these concerns. "You referred to being in Romania. Historically, there are things in

Romania that holy waters are useful tools against, and I am researching the effectiveness of different holy waters against these evils, if you catch my meaning." We maintained eye contact for an extended moment, my head nodding ever so slightly to communicate, "Yes, I am referring to vampires."

The Imam spoke. "There is great evil in the world, and then there are stories of evil that oftentimes are not true. It is very easy to get lost in both. I would suggest you take comfort in your own beliefs and spiritual tools, whatever they may be. If you are interested in learning more about Islam or the Sunni faith, I would be happy to assist you with that. However, concerning Abi Shifa water, I am afraid we have concluded our discussion on that."

I was disappointed, yet I also appreciated the Imam's delicate handling of my inquiry. I would have thought I was nuts and called for some psychiatric help if I were in his position, and I was glad he did not. I thanked him for his time, stood up, and shook his hand. I turned around to begin picking up the rug. "Oh, don't bother with that. Rasheed will come out and get these." The Imam then called for Rasheed, who was the other man he had been talking to when they arrived earlier. The Imam spoke to Rasheed, then turned to me and said "Good luck. ma'aasalaama." I thanked him again for his time, then he left and entered the mosque.

I turned my attention to Rasheed. "Are you sure I can't help you with these?"

Rasheed, who was bent down on the cement rolling the rug up, looked up at me and said "No, but I believe I can help you."

I didn't know what to say to Rasheed's comment, so I just stared back at him. Rasheed stood up and walked over to my rug, then repeated the same motions of rolling up the rug. Rasheed smiled at me and said, "The Imam is a great man; very gentle. He is correct though in his self-appraisal; he is very protective, and somewhat paranoid. I guess growing up the way he did *when* he did would make any of us that way."

I replied, "Yeah, I could see that."

Rasheed looked at me and said "But he is definitely, what do you Americans say, "Old School" when it comes to vampires."

I was startled with what Rasheed said. Rasheed leaned his head in the direction of the mosque. "Oh, I was listening to you inside the doorway there. I had some things to attend to there, so I wouldn't exactly call it eavesdropping. "Employing selective hearing" would be a better description." Rasheed smiled, stood up, threw both rugs over his shoulder, then took his loose hand and motioned for me to follow him.

We entered the mosque and turned down a hall to a room where many similar rugs were stored. Rasheed placed the rugs back on the shelf, then motioned for me to close the door. Once the door was closed, Rasheed began speaking. "So what is a nice American like you doing with vampires?"

I found myself speechless again. My mouth was open, and I could feel my eyes darting around trying to find the right thing to answer to this question. "Ahhh……" was all I could manage.

Rasheed laughed. "Are you trying out for a choir friend? We are Muslims, we don't have choirs."

I shut my mouth and smiled at how silly I must have looked. "No, I'm not trying out for a choir. This is something I'm just not used to talking about. When you're involved in something that most people don't believe in, you get good at keeping your mouth shut."

Rasheed smiled. "I am studying to be an Imam. The role I play is not as stringent as a Catholic priest, but many do talk to me about things they would not engage in conversation with others."

I decided to take Rasheed into my confidence; I had nothing to lose and possibly a few things to gain. I spoke in a somber tone. "To make a long story short, I am doing scientific experiments with vampire remains."

It was now Rasheed's turn to look surprised. He replied to this in a deadpan, yet serious tone. "Oh my. That is…..different. Most people I talk to about this are Dracula enthusiasts or something not as…..real. So you really do have vampire…….parts?"

"Teeth," I replied. "I have a set of vampire teeth." Rasheed opened his mouth to begin speaking, but I continued first. "They're genuine. I did quite a few tests on them to insure they were the real thing, and they are." Rasheed nodded his head. I could tell he was trying to get a grasp on what I had told him. "Yeah," I said, "and so I am conducting experiments on them to confirm or refute various vampire myths. This is why I came here today, to try and get some Abi Shifa water to test on the teeth since Abi Shifa water is a type of holy water."

Rasheed opened his mouth and nodded his head. "I see."

" It's the reason I came to Constanta. As I am sure you are already aware, Constanta is the most Muslim location in Romania. If I can't get the water here, then I'm going to have to leave Romania and try to acquire it in another country, and as an American…"

Rasheed interrupted me this time. "Yes, I could see where that could be a problem."

Then there was silence. I watched Rasheed scratch his hand, and maneuver his eyes much like other people do when considering ideas and options. "I can get it for you. It may be awhile, but I'll do it."

This surprised me. "Really? You'd do that? You don't even know me."

"No, I don't know you. And what you are telling me could all be an elaborate story. But on the other hand, you are standing here in a Mosque in a closet talking to me about this, so even if this is not true, I believe it very true to *you*, and if a pint of Abi Shifa water can bring you peace, then I, as an instrument of Allah, should help you with that. After all, Abi Shifa water is used for healing, so in a sense it would be being used for its intended purpose."

This was indeed a Godsend. If I let Rasheed get the Abi Shifa water, knew I would be sacrificing a level of quality control concerning the authenticity of the water. However, considering my other options, this was acceptable.

"I move around a lot to avoid the vampires, but I do have a mailbox in one town. That would be the best way to get it to me. I wouldn't need much, no more than the average size drinking water bottle."

Rasheed nodded. "It may be awhile, but I will eventually get some to you."

I asked if he wanted any money for this kind service. He put his hand up in a halting gesture. "If you want to give me something to cover the cost of shipping the water, that would be fine, but nothing more is needed. Money clouds purity, and this is something that would benefit from as much purity as possible."

We left the rug closet and I gave Rasheed my postal address and some money for the shipping costs. I was elated to have him helping me with this, and it felt good to have an ally who knew what I was doing. Even though he would be hundreds of miles from me, I didn't feel so alone with this anymore.

I asked if he would like to go to lunch. He declined, saying he would love to know more about what I was studying, but it may be best if we keep our personal contact to a minimum to divert suspicion from the Imam and whomever else may be watching me as a "person of interest." Rasheed smiled and then said "Besides, you're purpose here in Constanta is done. Go be a tourist!" Saying that, he made a shooing motion with his hands, as if I were a child being sent outside to recess.

I embraced Rasheed and said Namaste, which was the only term I knew in Arabic to say good-bye. He said Namaste also, and I left the Mosque. I couldn't tell if my shoes were noisy or not as I was floating on Cloud 9. Somewhere bells rang in the noon hour, and I thought about what Rasheed had said about being a tourist. All too soon, I would be going back to my laboratory. This, plus Rasheeds advice, as well as a feeling inside myself to celebrate solving the Abi Shifa water conundrum, I decided to relax and enjoy the rest of my afternoon in Constanta.

I went on a spree of shopping, sightseeing, and eating. I went back to the hotel about 7pm. Inside the lobby, one of the hotel clerks ran over to me with a piece of paper in his hand. "Excuse me Sir. Someone dropped this off for you."

I thanked the clerk and gave him a tip. I dropped my bags from my shopping and opened the envelope, which was the size of a personal note envelope and nice linen paper. The paper inside the envelope was equally fine, and said one sentence:

"So Mr. Cale, you are a scientist."

Oh shit.

I was back in my room figuring out my options. The vampires would be coming for me, and the way I saw it I had two options. The first was to endure the night here in the hotel. I had ample enough items for protection; I was hoping the myth that vampires had to be invited into your residence would apply to this hotel room. On the other hand, I could make a break for it and get on the train home before the sun went down. But what if one of their humans intervened on their behalf; someone did bring the note to me here at the hotel during daylight hours, after all.

I decided to stay at the hotel and take the train in the morning. If one of their humans followed me then, I would have the entire day to observe and deduce who was following me on the train. I would also have ample time to figure out a plan on how to get rid of them. The one thing I would have then, which I didn't have much of now, is time.

The cleaning staff had made my bed and addressed the common chores for the room, but had left the garlic cloves where I had left them from the night before. I chuckled to myself, thinking of an old cleaning woman tending to my room. Having noticed the garlic and understanding why it was there, she would either appreciate the meaning of my precautions or think the room guest a nut.

Dusk happened in an hour with total night darkness in two. The sun would rise at 5:30, so I figured I had approximately 9 hours of possible vampire interaction.

Humans working for the vampires would be a different story, but I assumed that since no one had tried to kill me since arriving at the hotel, they had been instructed not to approach me. In the morning, if their attempts had been unsuccessful, they may be unleashed to kill me, but I would much rather take my chances with humans in the daylight then vampires at night.

I went through possible scenarios concerning the vampire attacks. I deduced that the key thing they would be targeting on would be getting into my room, or getting me out of it. I had never heard of a vampire using fire before, so I ruled that out. Water didn't make much sense either since I was so far up in the building. Smoke was a possibility, but a weak one as that returned them to the idea of their employing fire against me. They could turn off the electricity to my room. Vampires, however, although brilliant, were not typically technology-oriented, and I was pretty sure the electrical grid for a hotel this size would have had a few computers designed to monitor it.

Then I considered a scenario that horrified me. What if the vampires tortured people in the hallway until I exited my room? That did sound like something vampires would do without any hesitation. What would I do if I heard people screaming in pain because I didn't act? How many people could I endure listening to be tortured?

Sadly, and perhaps selfishly, I resolved inside myself that if such a scenario were to develop, I could not leave the room. I was working on something that would benefit all of humanity, possible for centuries to come. My own self-preservation be damned, what I had discovered about vampires thus far was of paramount importance to the human race, and I had to preserve it, no matter the possible costs.

I was full from the meal I had eaten before coming back to the hotel. I had a few sodas left over from the night before, and there were still some coffee pods with the mini coffee maker. I went through my head to think of anything else I may need, but nothing came to mind. Nope, this was just going to come down to perseverance and, more than likely, sheer dumb luck.

I left the curtains open to watch the sunlight slowly fade away. Under normal circumstances, it would have been beautiful to watch. I tried to retain that attitude as I looked out the window, but sometimes there is only so much denial a person can generate.

Eventually, the sunlight completely evaporated and it was dark outside. Nothing had happened during the dusk period. It was hellacious being this anxious! I knew what not to do, but at the same time, I didn't know *what* to do. The idea of sitting around watching TV waiting for the neighborhood vampire society to come knocking on my door didn't feel like a great scenario to be in. Neither did getting a bath or going to sleep. Thought about reading, but that didn't sound that attractive either.

Then as thought occurred to me. If this was going to be my last night alive, what better way to spend it then enjoying life. I grabbed my laptop and connected to the hotel Wi-Fi. I went to Facebook, created an account, and looked up Felicity's page. It made me smile when I saw her profile picture with the account. I reviewed her photos from her trip. She appeared to be enjoying her journey; so many photos of her smiling brightly with great European backgrounds behind her.

I thought about contacting Yuri, my roommate from Brasov who educated me about the truth of the vampires, but decided against it. Yuri was working in conjunction with the Catholic Church and the vampire hunters, and they were far from enthusiastic about my entering the vampire equation. My research would have helped the hunters most of anyone, but after eons of doing things there way, the Church was stubborn about changing things.

I also thought about contacting Rasheed. This I

decided against as well. He was doing me an incredible favor, and it would have been nice to continue our conversation, but we had just met today. In the future, if I *had* a future, I might possibly contact him. For now though, Rasheed had experienced enough of vampires and me for one day.

I clicked off of Facebook and accessed my email account. There weren't many messages as I rarely used this account. I started typing a note to my father. Our relationship was not much more than one would have with someone you had met during a golf outing, but he was financially supportive of my "studies" as long as I stayed clean and sober. Since quitting drugs, I had been absorbed by my research, rarely communicating to anyone. I thought this was a wise approach, to keep everyone away from me as either to protect them or myself from the vampire world. In hindsight, even though my motive was good, I was not sure it was the best way to had gone about it.

I composed an email that described Romania and Constanta. He had often suggested coming over to visit me, but I always told him that he should stay in the States. Part of this was logical; he has a few medical concerns. Really though, he probably could have handled the trip. In reality, I just didn't want him over here getting in the way of my partying, then my research.

I had apologized for the emotional torment I had put him through when I was using drugs many times. This time, though, I took the opportunity to tell him that I was really trying to prove my worth as a good son by working on my science experiments to make him proud of me. I also said that I hoped very soon he could come to Romania, or maybe I could come back to the States for a visit, something I was scared to do because my drug use seemed to flourish on American soil.

I clicked on the send button. Then I closed my eyes and took a deep breath. Mom had left us years ago, her abandoning me one of the reasons I turned to dope. Now that I was clean, I could see so many paradigms that I couldn't see when I was on drugs. I was never able to feel compassion for my Dad; I was too busy feeling sorry for myself. I deeply regretted that, and I could hide behind my research to an extent, but I also felt I had to start doing more as a son.

Then I fell asleep.

A knock at the door woke me up. "Room service."

I got up to look out the security eyehole in the door. No one was in the hallway. I heard the knock again. "Room service." The knock wasn't coming from the hallway door, but behind me at the patio door. I turned

Vampirology

around to see Omar on my patio.

He knocked on the glass door again. "Room service".

They had arrived. I walked towards the glass window, but then I heard a knocking at the hallway door. "Room service." I went back to look out the eyehole again, this time seeing two people there, whom I assumed, since Omar was here, to be vampires.

I turned around again to look at Omar. "He knocked again. "Room Service."

I walked into the middle of the room. I retorted to Omar in a deadpan tone "I didn't order any room service."

"Mr. Cale, you are confused. You are *our* room service."

Oh shit.

I spoke to Omar. "Only if I open those doors. You would have attacked me by now if you could have, and you haven't. "

Omar responded. "We can't come in and you can't come out. It appears we are going to have a very interesting evening with each other."

I felt my inner-asshole start to come to the surface. "Would you like me to turn the TV towards the window so you can watch something out there? I'll have to turn the channels for you because I can't give you the remote, but that's OK. It's the least I can do for you for buying me coffee the other night."

I could tell Omar did not like my new tone. "You are going to die tonight, you know that."

Now I was angry. "Sorry, don't know that show. I'm afraid you're just going to have to just have to sit and wait out there." I walked over to the patio curtain strings, which put me two feet from Omar. The only thing stopping him from killing me was two panes of glass and a mystic spell. I pulled the curtain string and closed the curtains. I walked back to my bed, feeling as cocky and self-assured as I had felt the last time I went toe to toe with a vampire back in Brasov.

Knocking came from the patio and hallway doors. "Room service."

Knock, knock, knock. "Room service."

Knock, knock, knock. "Room service."

Knock, knock, knock. "Room service."

Knock, knock, knock.

I tried to ignore the noise my undead neighbors were making, but to no avail. I turned the TV on, but I could still here them. I turned the TV up as loud as it would go, but I could still hear them. It didn't surprise me that vampire voices worked on different decibel wavelengths than atypical human sounds, but it would have made my evening much easier if they would have been the same. I turned down the TV; no point having the human neighbors in the hotel rooms bothered with a blaring television from someone trying to drown out vampires.

I took out my laptop, got some music going, and tried to drown out the vampires with music in my headsets. That didn't work either, but I did have a bit of fun trying to find the right song to blend with the voices. It took a while, and I managed to find a song that would fit: Jim Croce's *Time in a Bottle*. Listening to a song about how your life has a finite amount of time with vampire background singers whose goal is to deliver the finality of your finite life didn't help things.

The vampires were still knocking two hours after they started. (I will have to say this for vampires: they are a persistent bunch!) I sat there trying to figure out what I could do that would keep me balanced. I had expected there to be a level of chaos inside myself from this evening, but I had expected that to be more fear and panic. Now that I understood the vampires couldn't enter my room and this was going to be a battle of perseverance, I had to adjust my game plan.

I considered opening the curtains and interviewing Omar. Here was a live (well, *animated*) vampire just a few feet from me, and a discussion about certain things would have been an asset to my research. I decided against this though; he was a vampire with a goal, and it would have been foolish for me to interact with a being who had untold manipulative tools at his disposal. I recalled an old saying: "If you dance with the devil, you are going to get burned."

I thought about calling someone, but I could just hear the conversation. "Hey, it's great to hear from you! You need me to hold on while you let the room service guy in?" There was a chance that the vampire voices wouldn't be carried over the telephone signal, but it was illogical to take such a risk.

Then an idea struck me! I got up from the bed and grabbed one of the garlic bulbs I had hung near the hotel door. I took the garlic bulb, separated the bulb into cloves, cleaned the cloves as best I could, and stuck the cleaned bulbs into my ears. I didn't hear the voices anymore! I was so geeked out by my discovery I started doing a little tap dance in the hotel room!

The scientist in me wanted to try to learn how this

garlic clove experiment worked in the realm of science, but I didn't know how to. Since this experiment worked, I formulated another vampire-sound experiment. I took the cloves of garlic out of my ears; the vampire "room service" song return clear and crisp when I did. I grabbed the cross that was by my bedside. Looking at the base of the crucifix, I realized that it was too big to insert into my ear. Instead, I put the cross besides my head by my ear to see if the crucifix would generate any static or interference to the vampire's voices. It did not.

I altered my next experiment by taking a knife to the center of the base of the crucifix to make wood shards that *would* fit into my ears. I put the garlic cloves back into my ears as I did this as manipulating the knife on the wood proved harder than I expected. It would have been easier to create a splinter-sized shard, but I wanted something that I wouldn't lose in my ear.

It took some crafty knife manipulating, but I was able to get a 1/2'" piece of wood from the cross. I washed off the shard of any wood dust and rounded the ends; I didn't want to stab my ear, after all. After concluding these motions, I removed one of the garlic cloves and inserted the wood shard. The shard worked just as effectively as the garlic clove!

I looked around my hotel room in silence, loving every

minute of it. Then a thought came into my head: After shoving a wood shard from a crucifix and a garlic clove in my ears, I wouldn't be able to take the q-tip warning about not using q-tips in your ear canals seriously ever again.

So now there was silence. In some ways, the silence was eerier than hearing the vampires. Hearing them outside my room meant they were *outside* my room. In the silence, though, my own paranoia created my terror. I sat with my legs straightened on the bed, trying to figure out how to proceed with the night. I could try to get some sleep, but would that be wise with the conditions I was in? On the other hand, would it be better for me to have some rest before I go up against the vampire's humans? After all, the vampires seem to be held at bay outside the room, and with the addition of my garlic ear plugs, I didn't even hear them anymore. In the morning, though, the vampire's servants could be a greater threat to me.

It was odd thinking that my own species would be more dangerous to me than vampires would. Would vampire deterrents repulse vampire servants? I had never heard that belief or suggestion before, however, I remembered a line from a movie I saw some time back: "Just because I don't believe in it doesn't mean it isn't real." I decided to keep this hypothesis as a third-tier defense.

I realized the weakest part of my interaction with the servants would be my leaving this room. Once I was in the lobby, my chances for safety increased with the addition of more humans, especially if I alerted the hotel staff to some possible security issues. There was my answer!

I took a garlic clove from my ear and called the front desk. The vampires were still knocking, but this call was important. Within a few rings, the front desk clerk answered.

"Hello, front desk here."

I told the clerk that I would be checking out in the morning and that I would require every porter they had available when I left my room. He said he felt that two porters could do the job. I told the clerk that I was apprehensive about leaving the room and wanted people around me for my own mental stability. Then I told him I would give $30 tips to each porter or staff person who arrived to assist me in the morning.

"Oh, well then, I per your request, I will have every available person sent to your room at dawn. If I may say so sir, your tip allowance is most generous, and many people here would like the opportunity to earn such a tip. Is there a maximum of people whom you would like to assist you?"

I tried to talk in a regular tone, even though I was elated with the question he asked. "Well, I understand that a lot of your staff have families and are college students who could use the extra cash, so let's make it 10, no, 15 people. Yes, 15 people would be just great." I thought maybe that many staff people would be too many, but better to error on the side of caution. Besides, what I said was true; they could all use the cash.

The clerk asked in a quizzical tone "Fifteen people to assist one guest with their luggage. Are you sure you want this many people sir?"

I assured the clerk I was in my right mind with this request. "I had a few people yesterday try to assault me and I would feel more comfortable with people around me while I was leaving the hotel."

The clerk tried to convince me that the hotel was safe and that hotel security would stop such people from entering the hotel. I told him I was sure the security for the hotel was excellent, that this was for my own emotional and mental satisfaction.

"Very well sir. You will have fifteen of our staff at your door at dawn tomorrow."

I asked the clerk to insure there was a cab available when I left, then I thanked the clerk before hanging up.

Vampirology

Then I thought about the sight I would see in the morning through the eyehole. Where there once were two vampires there would now be fifteen eager staff people.

It was comforting to know I had my transport issue taken care of, but I still had the issue of what to do with the remaining hours of the night with the vampires. The relief from my morning safety concerns and the vampire "room service" chorus made me relax and tiredness came on me fast. Then an epiphany struck me: the sunlamp in the bathroom! If I slept in the bathroom tonight with the door locked and the sunlamp on, this would be two extra layers of protection again the vampires, who thus far and been unable to enter the room in the first place.

I got up from the bed, grabbed the sheets, pillows, and other assorted bedding items and dragged them into the bathroom. I also grabbed the alarm clock from bedside the bed and plugged it into the bathroom socket. The tub was dry, and the sunlamp was above the shower enclosure, so I elected to make my make shift nest in there.

As I nestled in the glass-enclosed shower under a

very cozy sunlamp, I thought about how a day ago, I had considered sleeping in this shower to avoid the vampires. At that time, I elected to sleep in the bed, my arrogance saying to the universe "come and get me!" A day later, here I was, exactly where I said I wouldn't be. I heard myself say, "You may be the leading vampire scientist in the world Steve, but never forget in the end, you are a human being trying to save his ass against vampires." With that thought, I went to sleep.

The alarm woke me up from a deep sleep. In atypical fashion, I reached over to try to hit the snooze button, instead hitting my hand against the glass wall of the shower. That slight thud woke me up quick as I remembered where I was and why I was there. I screened the bathroom for any differences; I did not see any.

The alarm said 530 A.M. I rose from my bathtub bed, slipping once on the slick surface where the sheets met the porcelain tub. As I tried a second time to get up, I thought to myself "That'd be about right. I survive a night against three vampires and break my neck getting out of my bathtub bed. The staff would come in, find me dead, see the bed I had constructed in the tub, and wonder what kind of nut job I must have been!"

I stopped the alarm, left the bathroom, and meandered towards the curtain. I could see some light sneaking in at the base of the curtain, so I knew the sun was up. I pulled the curtain string. A beautiful sunrise on the sea appeared; no vampire was there. I turned around to look out the eyehole in the door; no vampires there either. I took the garlic cloves from my ears. I heard the ventilation system of the hotel running, and nothing else.

I returned to the patio door. I scanned the patio one more time to insure I had not missed anything, then unlocked the door. A slight salty breeze met me as I slid the patio door open. I walked out onto the patio, leaned against the railing, and looked around at the magnificence of the day that was emerging. I took long, deep breaths of that salty air, never so happy to be breathing such a wonderful aroma in my life. Part of me could have spent the day out on that patio enjoying every part of life that scene could deliver, but I knew this was just a brief recess in the day I had in front of me.

I looked around the patio to see if there was anything to indicate that a vampire had been on the porch all night. Nothing looked different from the day before. I looked over the edge of the railing down to the ground; Omar had traveled quite a way up to visit last night.

One of the things I had done last night during the vampire chorus was I had gotten all my bags together for my departure this morning. I was ready to go. All I needed was for my mini-army to arrive and escort me to the cab. A cup of coffee would have been wonderful, but there would be time enough for such things on the train ride home.

Home. I laughed at myself with that word. Here I was in a posh hotel with a beautiful view of the sea, and all I wanted was to get back to my different lab locations in the shittier parts of a city. However, that was home now, and although it lacked a great many things most people take for granted, I just wanted to be back safe and secure in my lab.

There was a knock at the door. A different knock than the monotonous rapping the vampires had serenaded me with, and I enjoyed hearing it. An accented voice came from the door. "Porter service here sir." I looked through the eyehole to see fifteen people in the hallway. Some were porters, others had on the white clothes dishwashers and kitchen staff wore. I licked my lips and smiled as I opened the door to my hotel task force.

My hotel task force walked me from my room to the elevator. I could see from the looks in the eyes of more than a few of them that they did not understand why they were there. I had to have looked like a paranoid American tourist who was afraid the Bogeyman was going to get him; the events from the night before made this description all too accurate.

I was in the middle of the men and women who comprised my security detail. As we walked down the hall, I smelled the cologne from the porters, a perfume from one of the women from the front desk, and a greasy food smell from some of the kitchen staff. None of them talked during our stroll down the hallway, the only sounds being a muffled march as so many feet walked down the all at once.

My mind went back to all the video games I had played in my youth. I expected vampires to jump out of the doorways of the guest rooms we passed, of for some zombie squadron to fall through the ceiling panels to annihilate us. If only we could make it to the elevator, a common place in attack games for grenade launchers, laser guns, and other assorted armaments. It was silly to think this way, but a night of vampire-induced sleep deprivation does play with your mind.

The elevator doors slid open and we all piled inside. It was tight, but even though we were all jammed together in the elevator, I felt as snug and secure as a baby in a blanket. The odd part was being in an elevator with so many people and everyone being so *quiet.* I could hear the grunts and groans of the old lift as it delivered all of us to the ground floor.

On the ground floor, the doors opened and we all exited the elevator, all of us still very close together. It was hard for me to get a view of how many people were in the lobby and front desk area, and those I was able to get a glimpse of did not look like vampire servants. (It was at this time I heard a voice in my head say "And just what does a vampire servant look like, Steve? You're the one who had a vampire come up and stand next to you on the seashore without knowing he was a vampire; how the hell are you going to tell who is a vampire servant?!")

We walked through the hotel and towards the main entry. I said, "Stop" before we went through the sliding glass doors. One of the women who were wearing the delicate perfume was to my right. I pointed to her and motioned for her to come with me over a few feet from the sliding door. The professionally dressed woman acquiesced with my request and walked towards me. I pulled out my wallet and took out a $500 traveler's check, which I had signed the night before. I handed her the traveler's check and instructed her in Romanian

"Take this over to the front desk clerk and get the money for everyone. Please dispense the money to the staff here and give the rest to some of the cleaning staff and front desk staff." (I thought since I had left all of my bedding in the bathroom, the least thing I could do is throw a little tip money their way.) She nodded in agreement and did what I requested. She put her arm in the air with the check held high and said "follow me" to my makeshift security staff. I waved good-bye to them, walked through the sliding doors, and got into a cab that was waiting for me just as I had instructed. I instructed the cab driver to take me to the train station. While he pulled away from the hotel, I looked backwards to see if we were being followed by car or someone on foot; nothing looked out of the ordinary from what would be an otherwise developing downtown scene. I turned back around, took a long deep breath of the evergreen air-freshened air, and thought about how grateful I was to have survived the night.

The train station looked so different than it did when I arrived just a few days ago. Nothing in the physical appearance of the station had changed, but what the building symbolized to me certainly had! There were many people here and there around the station, but I wouldn't call it crowded either. Most of the people had some sort of baggage; I didn't think a vampire servant would be after me with a set of luggage by their side.

The air smelled of the sea and diesel, and although I did like the perfume of the woman from the hotel, this had a specific aroma to my soul, a smell of survival and escape. Out of nowhere in my brain came a song lyric *"I pulled into Nazareth, feeling about half past dead..."* I could relate.

After checking in at ticket counter, I sat down on one of the benches near the door to the train. I looked around at all of the people in the station again; no one alerted me to possible danger. Maybe I was making too big of a deal of this. Paranoia with the vampires last night was just good thinking, but this was different. Here was just a bunch of people going about their business to get to where they needed to go. Nothing happened at the hotel when I was leaving, and I hadn't seen anyone following me from the hotel either.

I was just about to relax when I saw a cab deliver two men in their twenties who were all wearing black leather and more than a few face piercings. I watched this crew enter the station and scan the station as if they were looking for someone. One of the men looked

V a m p i r o l o g y

at me, tilted his head, and then elbowed the fellow next to him. The other guy looked over at me, said something to the first guy, then both men nodded in agreement.

Now it was time to cowboy up; the "daylight demons" had arrived…

They knew I had seen them, yet they did not come over to me. Instead, they sat on the opposite side of the station, all the while facing me. It was an odd position to be in. Here were these two notorious looking men, the kind of guys you would have crossed the street to avoid, yet they did not move against me. Did I garner that much respect and awe? My ego would have liked to embrace that fallacy, but I wasn't that arrogant, or stupid. I continued to look at the men, putting my fingertips together in a contemplative gesture. People meandered between us, human pieces moving around an invisible chessboard between my newfound rivals and me.

As a test, when the announcer said that one of the trains was preparing to leave, I rose from my place, grabbed my bag, and began walking away from the seating area. The two men got up from their seats and began walking in the same direction as I had moved. I stopped in front of a vending machine and pretended to look over the selections. The two followers stopped at the end of the seats and spoke amongst themselves while maintaining a view of me at the machine.

Then it struck me; they didn't know what train I was getting on! That would explain why they hadn't bought any tickets yet. I looked at the train schedules on the monitor. There were a few trains leaving before my train was set to depart. Maybe I could use this to my advantage…

I looked around the station. I saw a lady with three kids under the age of 10 near the door to one of the platforms. The kids were not hyper, but active, obviously bored with waiting for the train. The lady, who looked like SHE had been the one dealing with vampires all night, tried to maintain the kids as best she could. The train she was waiting for was one of the trains that were going to depart before mine.

I saw my chance. I went over to the lady with the kids and began a discussion. "Hi, looks like you got your hands full!" She looked up at me from her seat, opened her eyes wide, and nodded in agreement. Then I started putting on the BS. "My sister has three kids, and she has to travel by herself a lot too. Could you use a hand getting the kids and your stuff on the train? I'd be happy to help; it'd make me feel better for all the times I wish I would have been available to help my sister with her kids?" Yes, it was a bold face lie, but I had a plan for getting rid of the daytime demons, and being of help to his family was an important part of it.

A large glass window separated the loading area from the passenger waiting area. I sat down on the cement and leaned against the glass. The daylight demons stayed their distance, watching me from afar. They had not approached me yet, and I doubted they would do so now that I was near a mother and kids. Romanian people would react if there were a ruckus around a mom and her kids; they are very protective that way.

I asked the two kids if I could play with them; has any kid ever said no? They brought their cars over to where I was sitting. The polished concrete floor made for an excellent roadway for the miniature cars. I slid a toy car around, driving "in-drift" style like in the Fast & Furious movies, making all the sound effects possible as I maneuvered the toy around. The kids laughed at my sounds, and I had to admit I was having a good time playing with them.

The boy's name was Ramon and the little girl was Louisa. He was 5 and she was 4; both made sure to put their little fingers in the air to illustrate to me the right amount of years with their hands. He had a short-buzzed haircut while Louisa had long curls that most women would die for.

I had just grabbed my bag to make a mountain for us to drive up when the announcement came that the train was ready for boarding. I asked the kids if they wanted to hold my hands as I helped walk them and their mom to the train, looking to their mom for approval as I did so. The kids grabbed my hands, and we teetered off towards the train, mom and baby an arm's distance from all three of us.

I looked over at my pursuers as we started towards the train. They did not move, they just continued to watch me. An odd feeling crept into my body as I walked with the kids while being eyed by the vampire servants: this is the reason I do what I do. These kids, these people, they deserve protection against these vermin, these parasites. The human race, despite all of our flaws, can be beautiful, and I was so grateful that I had these kids holding my hands to remind me of this. I felt so on fire with this newfound passion for my research, part of me wanted to let go of the kids, go over to the daylight demons, and start a fight. (Good thing the kids *were* holding my hands!)

The sliding door opened and we were met with the cool diesel-scented air of the loading dock. The loading area between the train and the building created a small wind corridor, and a slight but regular breeze flowed through the walkway. Some of the other patrons had left the passenger area before us and were lined up to board the train at an entry where a conductor stood.

Once we got into the line to get on the train, I noticed the demons coming out onto the loading platform. They did not get in line with us though, as we were the last in line. They had been maintaining a regular distance from me since their arrival and were maintaining the same distance from me on the loading ramp. (The scientist in me was curious to know why they were acting the way they were and whether they were instructed to do this or if there was another motivating reason.)

As we were walking in line, I told the kids about the engine in the front of the train and some other little things about the train. I don't know whether it was being useful to someone, the kids holding my hands, or the sunlight from the emerging day, but I felt wonderful! I was so content, I felt as if I were floating above the cement loading dock!

When we got to the conductor, I told him that I was just helping the lady behind me with getting her kids onto the train and that my train would be leaving in a few minutes on another track. The conductor nodded in understanding and let the kids and me onto the train.

The three of us waited for mom and baby in the dome where the drawbar connected the coach cars together. The conductor helped the mom up into the train. I let go of the kids and grabbed the bag the mom was carrying. She moved in front of me, leading the way to the compartment they had on their tickets.

Once we arrived at the compartment, I looked out the window. I could see the daylight demons were getting on the train. I couldn't tell what they told the conductor, or what the conductor said back.

I sat down in one of the seats and told the mom and kids I would stay here until the train departed from the station. The kids asked why I wasn't going with them. I had forgotten as a child, you want every relationship to last, everyone to go with you, and you never want anyone to leave. It warmed my heart to be asked this, but also saddened me that I had to tell them I had to go somewhere else. Louisa asked why I had to go. I told her some reason a 4-year-old would believe; I sure in the hell wasn't going to tell her the truth!

I turned my head towards the door to the compartment. The door has a window with a privacy shade that was up. I saw the demons pass by the window. We both recognized each other, both of us continuing to pretend that we didn't. I would have liked to known where they were going, or if they were getting into a compartment, but the dance steps of our dance had already been choreographed, and I wasn't going to change the dance we were dancing just yet.

The conductor knocked on the door and pointed to his watch. I caught his hint. I got up, gave both kids a hug. The mom, whose name I never did learn, gave me a hug as well and thanked me for helping her out with the kids. I reached into my pocket, grabbed my wallet, and gave the mom a $100 bill. She put her hand up, saying "No" many times. I told her that it wasn't for her, it was for my speeding tickets that I had accumulated from the police (Ramon and Louisa) while we were playing with the cars. Then I winked and gave her the bill.

To this day, I would have liked to known what happened to that family…

I exited the compartment into the hallway. I walked away from the direction the vampire servants walked, stopping in the dome area where we had loaded earlier. I stood in a position where I could look down the hallway I had just left and look out at the loading platform, my bag making a good cushion against the wall of the dome. I heard a lot of commotion all around me as the train ready to depart, but I didn't see anyone.

It was odd not knowing where the people who were following you were, and having an idea where they were didn't bring much solace. I couldn't tell if it was my lack of sleep, my own addictive paranoia, or the effect of too many schlocky horror movies messing with my head; looking back it was probably a combination of all three. I found myself breathing heavy, the anxiety of the moment mixing with the diesel fumes from the engine increasing power. All of this reminded me of the third day of my detox when I was sweating and had just went through the worst night of withdrawals. I felt terrible, but that memory increased my perseverance; if I could survive that misery, I could handle this!

The plan was simple: get the demons on this train, jump off the train, leave the demons on this train to deliver them to another place, get on my train. I was at the jumping off the train part, the part they make look so easy in the movies. Let me tell you, the idea of jumping 4 feet off a moving train, even a slow-moving train, is not easy! There are all sorts of pieces of conduit and other railroad junk to avoid while you are trying to jump; it's as if the railroad company wanted to construct an obstacle course to insure no one jumped off the train!

We kept moving ever so slowly. I still did not see the demons. When we were getting to the speed where the gravel under the tracks started to blur, I moved to the edge of the doorway to make my jump. I positioned my bag onto my right arm rather than my back, hoping to use the bag as a cushioning device for my landing. I grabbed a hold of the handrails people used to pull themselves into the train. I looked down the hallway one last time. I saw someone coming out of a compartment at the far end of car. It was hard to see if it was the demons or not, but then I saw a glimmer of silver from the hand of the person. I still couldn't confirm that it was them or not, but now was not the time to reposition myself to look. I counted one, two, three, and jumped.

I have done many crazy things in my life. Thus far, I have lived to tell about them. I can say with the utmost certainty that jumping off a moving train is something that, once you have done it, you will NEVER do it again. The movies that people do this is in are *ALL LIES*!

Let me begin by saying my bag on the arm idea didn't work. What it did do is put a major bruise on my arm when I impacted with the gravel and popped my shoulder in and out of place. In addition, when I landed, I grated my face against the gravel, which really wasn't gravel as much as shards of rock the size of my thumb.

The area between my eye and hairline down to my jaw was shred into human hamburger. The best part of the whole situation was hearing the train still running down the tracks and not seeing anyone else jump off the train, although I would not have minded the daylight demons experiencing what I was going thorough at that moment.

A station employee ran over from the loading dock to me and helped me up. "You ok?" I nodded that I was, my jaw hurting from the impact of the ground and the carnage that was now my face. The employee, a twenty-something fellow, assisted me back into the station restroom to wash my face. As we walked along the loading dock, I saw several people looking at me through the glass windows of the passenger area, no doubt wondering what in the hell just happened.

In the restroom, I get to see my face for the first time. Yeesh! It was gross. The station guy got me a wet paper towel to apply to my face, then told me he was going to go get a first aid kit. I tried to reach for the towel with my right hand, the fire in my shoulder screaming as more pain came with the movement of the arm. I altered my body and grabbed the towel with my left hand. The guy left for the first aid kit while I attended to my face. I dabbed at my wound as I looked in the mirror, saying words in English no gentleman would say in Romanian.

The fellow came back with the first aid kit. While he was opening the kit, he asked what had happened. I was ill prepared to answer this; I had not planned to damage myself and need attention from anyone. I closed my eyes and shook slightly shook my head, and then pointed to my face. The employee understood I didn't want to talk and proceeded to apply anti-septic jell to my wounds. It stunk a bit, the pain really coming when he used a small folded piece of paper towel to scrape a few small pieces of grit out of my face.

As time passed, various sore spots emerged as my body began to calm from the adrenaline boost from the jump. I wanted to sit down and look at my legs and other sore spots, but the restroom didn't have chairs, so I motioned for the employee to escort me to the passenger area. He grabbed my bag and we hobbled to the seating area. The employee steered me to the closest chair to the restroom, but I motioned that I wanted to go sit on the other side of the room. He looked at me confused, but acquiesced to my request. Some people looked at me, but most of them had returned to their own business. As I staggered to the place I wanted to sit, I studied the waiting area; I did not see the vampire servants. There was no way to insure the demons were still on the train I jumped from, but since I didn't see them in the room, I had to work on the assumption that they were still on that train. I couldn't drop my guard entirely, but a certain amount of ease came over me as I sat down.

The sunlight that had felt so good earlier when I was on the loading platform with the kids now made everything I had hurting more irritating. I leaned forward to pull my pant leg up to inspect the sore spots I was feeling, but the change in my body position poured gasoline onto the fire that was already in my shoulder.

The fellow that had helped me in the restroom asked me if I wanted him to take me to the hospital. In a perfect world, I would have gone to a hospital and had all my injuries tended to. Of course, in a perfect world, I wouldn't have been jumping off a running train to avoid vampire henchmen, either. I politely declined his offer and said I was just going to sit here and wait for my train.

My statement confused the employee. "But sir…. you were just on your train?" He pointed towards the area I had made my jump.

Talking just above a whisper, I told the employee "That's the reason I jumped off; I was on the wrong train."

The ride back to my lab was a living hell. My shoulder was on fire, and each bump or jostle made it impossible for me to get comfortable. If I was lucky to get into a position that didn't hurt my shoulder, then I was unable to put my face against anything from the ooze of the antiseptic gel and natural seepage from my wounds. (95% of the time, I was a very grateful ex-junkie. However, it was times like this I really regretted being a recovering addict! It would have been so nice to just pop a few pills and fade out of reality…)

I got back to the location I called Lab #1. My little military cot was still in the same corner where it was when I had left, and I was ever so glad to back in my little laboratory lair!

www.ingramcontent.com/pod-product-compliance
Lightning Source LLC
Chambersburg PA
CBHW071522170626
46811CB00007B/2928